"Do you have any idea how exceptional you are, Abby?" Webb asked.

"I'm not"—her breath caught as his hand caressed her throat and jaw until his thumb came to rest on her bottom lip—"exceptional," she finished. Her tongue darted out to moisten her suddenly dry lips and accidentally stroked the rough skin of his thumb.

A smoky haze came into his eyes as the mere touch of her sent liquid fire through his body. His hands cupped her face, holding her still. "You are exceptional, courageous, and the most beautiful woman I've ever known."

"You don't have to say things like that to me, Webb," she murmured seriously. "I know who I am and what I am."

His lips brushed lightly over hers. "You haven't the faintest idea who and what you are if you think I'm wrong." He pulled back to look at her then. "The ugly duckling has turned into a swan, but you've been too tired and busy to see it. You also can't see that I'm interested in you—in your life, your work, your thoughts, your feelings, everything about you." His hands slid down over her shoulders and moved over her body, his dark gaze fixed on her face. "Now don't pull away from me, Abby. I want to show you just how beautiful you are to me . . ."

WHAT ARE *LOVESWEPT* ROMANCES?

They are stories of true romance and touching emotion. We believe those two very important ingredients are constants in our highly sensual and very believable stories in the *LOVESWEPT* line. Our goal is to give you, the reader, stories of consistently high quality that may sometimes make you laugh, sometimes make you cry, but are always fresh and creative and contain many delightful surprises within their pages.

Most romance fans read an enormous number of books. Those they truly love, they keep. Others may be traded with friends and soon forgotten. We hope that each *LOVESWEPT* romance will be a treasure—a "keeper." We will always try to publish

LOVE STORIES YOU'LL NEVER FORGET
BY AUTHORS YOU'LL ALWAYS REMEMBER

The Editors

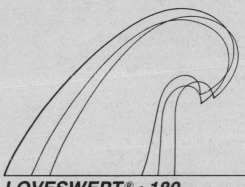

LOVESWEPT® • 180

Patt Bucheister
The Dragon Slayer

BANTAM BOOKS
TORONTO • NEW YORK • LONDON • SYDNEY • AUCKLAND

THE DRAGON SLAYER

A Bantam Book / February 1987

Cover art by Barnett Plotkin.

If you would be interested in receiving protective vinyl
covers for your Loveswept books, please write to this address
for information:

Loveswept
Bantam Books
P.O. Box 985
Hicksville, NY 11802

ISBN 0-553-21797-6

Published simultaneously in the United States and Canada

PRINTED IN THE UNITED STATES OF AMERICA

O   0 9 8 7 6 5 4 3 2 1

I would like to extend my thanks to Anita Ford, a docent (guide) at the eighteenth-century Lynnhaven House in Virginia Beach, Virginia, for her patience and generous sharing of her abundant knowledge.

One

"Move your tush out of the way, Betsy Ross. This man is injured."

Abigail Stout's tush stayed where it was. Ignoring the snide comment about the way she was dressed from the impatient man behind her, she snapped, "We're not exactly out for an afternoon stroll. My friend is hurt, too, so hold your horses. I'm trying to get the door open."

"Do you have problems with the word *push*?" the man drawled sarcastically.

For the third time, Abby slammed her hand against the square four-inch metal plate with PUSH engraved on it. The sliding glass door of the emergency room remained stubbornly closed. The modern curse words that came to mind didn't go with the eighteenth-century colonial costume she was wearing. Cursing didn't help. The blasted door refused to budge.

The man behind her spoke again. "Don't they have doors where you come from, Betsy?"

With her arm still supporting her co-worker, Brenda, Abby turned around. Two men were standing several feet away, dressed in dusty jeans and blue chambray shirts. Their clothing was covered with a fine film of the brown dirt from the clay soil of that area of Virginia. The shorter man was wearing a battered yellow hard hat and supporting one clumsily wrapped forearm with his other hand. The younger man, next to him, his hands resting on his slim hips, was obviously impatient.

Abby directed her glare at him, instinctively choosing the one who had been giving her a hard time. It was necessary to tilt her head back in order to look into his face. Not only was he tall, but he was dark and ruggedly handsome as well. He was also irritatingly rude.

"You have a nerve," she said, "making fun of the way I'm dressed, when you look like you've been rolling around in a barrow pit."

The man's stony expression didn't change except for a speculative gleam in his cool gray eyes. "Was I making fun of you?"

"You called me Betsy Ross. I would say that's making fun of the way I'm dressed."

A slight breeze ruffled his thick, coal-black hair. "Do you expect an apology?"

Abby had a feeling he was not the type of man who apologized or made excuses for any of his actions. His self-assurance was apparent in his voice and the way he stood, but she sensed it was from self-confidence rather than from arrogance.

"I expect common courtesy, that's all," she replied solemnly. Taking a step out of the way, she gestured to the metal plate on the door. "You seem to be the pushy type, so you shouldn't have any trouble pushing this door open. How about you moving *your* tush over here and trying to open the dumb door if you think it's so darn easy?"

His eyes narrowed while he studied her for a few seconds, as if he had just discovered something unique but didn't quite know what to make of it. Disconcerted by his unblinking stare, she added, "Since I don't plan to make opening this door my life's work, you had better give it a try, or we'll be here all day."

"Now, why didn't I think of that?" he drawled.

He reached around her, and his arm accidentally brushed her breast as he put his palm against the plate. With an irritating whoosh, the glass doors parted as if by magic.

Smiling smugly, he murmured, "It's hard getting used to these newfangled inventions, isn't it, Betsy?" Then he turned back to the man he had brought to the hospital. "Let's go, Turk."

Gritting her teeth to keep from screaming in frustration, Abby hustled Brenda through the entrance after the men had passed through. She didn't trust the door to stay open long.

"I wish I had fainted at his feet so he could pick me up," Brenda whispered, gazing at the tall man walking ahead of them.

Abby frowned. Her breast was still tingling from the brief contact with the man's arm. "He probably would have calmly stepped over you."

"Don't be such a grump, Abby. You love beautiful things, and, honey, that man is absolutely gorgeous."

"I never noticed," she lied gamely. "We came here to have that burn on your leg treated, remember?"

Once Brenda had been turned over to a nurse, Abby got a cup of coffee and headed for the waiting room. She needed a transfusion of caffeine to keep her going. The familiar weariness had seeped into her bones, but the day was only half over. There was still a lot to do. Standing in the hot August sun trying to open the door to this darn hospital had made her hot under the collar in more ways than one. She might as well use this time to relax.

Curious glances slid over her colonial costume as she sat down on one of the molded plastic chairs in the crowded waiting room. There hadn't been time to change into her regular clothing after Brenda had burned her leg during a cooking demonstration at Bristol House. Between putting out the flames licking Brenda's skirt and getting another docent to take over the demonstration, the last thing on Abby's mind had been how she looked.

But then, she gave very little thought to her looks most of the time. To her mind, there wasn't much to think about. When she had been much younger, she had hated her ordinary features. By now, at the age of twenty-five, she had come to terms with the fact that her face and figure would never stop traffic. It was some small consolation to know her looks weren't so bad that they would stop a clock, either.

Glancing around, Abby confronted a glare from a woman wearing an extremely tight T-shirt over a bra-less drooping bosom. Apparently the woman did not approve of Abby's outfit, but since the other woman's choice of apparel made her look like a sack of cantaloupes, Abby refused to let the woman's critical stare bother her. Everyone else appeared to be mildly amused and let it go at that.

Well, almost everyone.

Her earlier antagonist had entered the waiting room, taking up a position against one wall instead of sitting on a chair. He'd crossed his arms over his chest and was staring at her. His gaze roamed insolently over her long homespun skirt and the white apron tied around her slender waist. His inspection trailed up over the puff-sleeved white top of her shift before moving on to her reddish-blond hair, which was wound into a coil beneath her white mob cap. A few strands of her hair had come loose and framed her face.

She stared back at him defiantly, crossing her arms in imitation of his stance. What the heck? she thought. It certainly was no hardship to look at him, even if she was mainly challenging his rude stare. He was a fine specimen of manhood. If the woman in the tight T-shirt had an ounce of female hormones, she would be gawking at him instead of at Abby.

Webb Hunter's gaze didn't falter as he met the stormy eyes of the woman he had called Betsy Ross. A corner of his mouth lifted in amusement when he saw her chin raise slightly as she continued to stare him down. She was a spirited little thing, he thought, remembering their brief exchange outside the hospital. He had been impressed when she had stood up to him. Not many people did. Maybe that was why he had automatically looked for her when he came into the waiting room. She was refreshingly different, and it wasn't just because of her odd costume.

Usually a woman's physical attributes caught his eye—and held his attention—but this woman's conversation had had a spice and flavor that fit his taste, a taste he'd never known he had until now. His eyes narrowed as he remembered his body's reaction to the feel of her breast when he had grazed against it earlier. He still found it unbelievable. Good Lord, he was an experienced thirty-five-year-old, not a virginal fifteen. So why the disturbing sensation that he'd experienced something new? How ridiculous! He had certainly touched a woman more intimately before without half the reaction he had had when barely touching this woman.

Abby was wondering how much longer she could stare back at this suddenly fierce-looking man, when the elderly woman sitting next to her tapped her arm. She turned her head, thereby breaking eye contact. The woman asked about her costume, and Abby explained that she was a guide at Bristol House. A number of people in the Tidewater area, particularly those interested in history, knew about the historical significance of Bristol House. The woman sitting next to Abby was one of them. The eighteenth-century house was open to visitors during the summer months, displaying the architecture, furniture, crafts, and skills of that earlier time. The guides in period costume often demonstrated various household tasks. The previous week there had been a mock Civil War battle on the grounds, performed by groups of Civil War buffs, dressed in blue and gray uniforms.

One of the women sitting across from Abby leaned forward to listen intently as Abby described how she had made her costume by hand, as it would have been made in the eighteenth century. Caught up in her subject, she went on to talk about some of the customs of the period, as she did for visitors to Bristol House. Soon several people had put down their magazines or stopped watching television to listen to what Abby had to say.

From across the room, Webb couldn't hear what the oddly dressed woman was saying, but he couldn't take his eyes off her. He hadn't the faintest idea why he kept looking at her. She wasn't the type of woman who usually appealed to him. His female companions were more polished, with stunning figures and beautiful faces made more attractive by expertly applied makeup. This strange creature appeared to have been transported from another age.

One of the pink-uniformed volunteers appeared in the doorway of the waiting room. She gazed around the room as she inquired, "Mr. Hunter?"

Webb pushed away from the wall. "I'm Hunter."

"Will you come with me, please?"

Even though she continued talking to her small group of interested listeners, Abby watched the man named Hunter as he strode toward the door. It was pure pleasure just to watch him walk. He looked as good from the back as he did from the front. There was no doubt about it; blue jeans had been designed with his physique in mind. Slender hips, long legs, a graceful walk like a stalking wildcat.

Mentally giving herself a shake, Abby brought her attention back to the elderly woman beside her. She was sharing an anecdote about the Civil War, something about how the Yankees had come to her ancestor's home and used a wardrobe cabinet as a watering trough for their horses. A hoofprint was still impressed on the wooden door, which had been torn off before the wardrobe was filled with water.

Abby's mind continued to slip back to the dark-haired man, even though he was no longer in the room. It was a sign of how tired she was, she told herself, for her thoughts to be dwelling on a stranger, a man she would never see again. It was a harmless enough diversion, but a waste of time.

Time. When had time become her enemy? There just wasn't enough of it in a day. Between attending classes at the local college two mornings a week, working at the colonial house in the afternoons, and playing piano in a hotel lounge each night, Abby used up time at a fast pace. There was little of it left for such things as rest or relaxation. Still, she wasn't getting everything done fast enough to suit her. She had hoped to have her master's degree by the time she was twenty-five, but she hadn't made it. She'd had her twenty-fifth birthday four months ago, and had a few more weeks of work yet to do on her thesis. A quarter of a century had gone by and she still had not reached her goal. Working two jobs took up so much time, hours she could be spending on her thesis, but she needed to work. Her rent had to be paid.

Once the thesis was completed and she had her master's degree, everything she had hoped for, planned for, and worked for would fall into place. All she had to do was keep up her heavy schedule for a little while longer.

The elderly woman was called to the reception desk, and gradually the others returned to their magazines or left. The mini-history lesson was over.

A rush of fatigue flowed through Abby's weary body. She took a sip of coffee, then leaned her head against the wall behind her and closed her eyes. All she had to do was keep going, she repeated silently. It sounded so easy, but it was becoming harder to do.

Since she had her eyes closed, she didn't see Webb Hunter return to the waiting room. If she had, she would have noticed he was not a happy man. Irritated by the news of a further delay before Turk could leave the hospital, Webb was chafing at the constriction put on his time. Upon entering the waiting room, he became even more annoyed when he realized he had immediately looked to see if the woman in the colonial costume was still there. He felt absurdly pleased that she was. His sharp gaze took in her closed eyes and the mauve shadows underneath them. He wondered why she looked so exhausted. Too many late nights? What did he care how she spent her nights? Or why she was dressed so strangely? It shouldn't matter to him one way or the other what she did with her time. It was none of his business.

Unlike her, he had work to do, and he couldn't get much accomplished standing around in the waiting room. He was late for an appointment with a building inspector, who would be out at the job site and away from a phone. He had called his secretary to let her know where he was, in case the inspector phoned, wondering what had happened. She would explain the emergency, but Webb hated looking inefficient. It was a lesson he had learned early in life. If you say you're going to do something, you'd damn well better do it. There were two things he had no tolerance for: inefficiency and irresponsibility . . . and at the moment he knew he appeared to be guilty of both.

If it had been anyone else but Turk, he would have ordered one of the other men to bring the injured man to the hospital. Turk had been with Webb's construction company since it started, though, and was one of the few people Webb allowed close enough to be a friend. It wasn't that he didn't like people. He was selective. He preferred quality in friends, not quantity.

Webb began to pace the room to release some of the impatience boiling up inside him. Several people moved their feet out of his way as he passed, and one woman picked up her child, who had been playing on the floor. One look at his thunderous expression was enough to convince people to stay out of his way. It was too bad Abby didn't see it.

She was blissfully unaware of the danger her feet were in until a heavy work boot tromped on one of them. Her eyes flew open at the same time that her Styrofoam cup tilted and coffee spilled on her lap. She exclaimed loudly at the sudden pain in her foot, drawing the attention of most of the other people in the waiting room.

The man named Hunter was the first thing she saw. The blank, impersonal look in his eyes wasn't much help in determining what had just happened. He was standing almost on top of her, though, his booted foot planted only inches from her throbbing one, and it didn't take an Einstein to figure it out. The blasted man had stepped on her foot! Did he look sorry? Was there a glimmer of apology or regret in his cool gray eyes? No. He was looking down at her as if she were a chair he had just bumped into.

So much for tea and sympathy, she thought. Maybe if she hadn't been so tired, his lack of compassion wouldn't have bothered her. Nor would tears be welling in her eyes. She never cried. It was a self-indulgence she wouldn't allow herself, but one look at the hard face of the man who had trounced on her toes and she was in danger of giving herself a pity party. A small corner of her mind wondered whether he would have the same bland reaction if she had been a curvaceous cutie who fluttered her eyelashes, instead of a plain Jane with bloodshot eyes.

Webb saw the glistening moisture and pain in her eyes just before she closed them for a fleeting moment. When she reopened them, a steely determination and pride had replaced any sign of vulnerability.

Her chin came up. Pointing to her other foot, she snapped, "You missed one."

Realizing what he had done, Webb took the cup out of her hand before any more coffee was spilled on her, and sat down beside her. "Are you all right?" he asked.

Expecting to see her foot squashed flat, Abby was reassured when she looked down to see that it was still attached to her ankle and fairly normal-looking. The silver buckle on the soft leather slipper was a little lopsided, but her foot seemed to be intact. She lifted it to her knee and gently rubbed it. "Did a steamroller just pass by, or was that you?"

His guilt at hurting her took the form of anger. "If you got some sleep at night, you would be aware of what's going on around you instead of dozing off in the middle of the day. Been staying up late sewing the flag, Betsy?"

Preoccupied with the pain in her foot and a strange awareness of his closeness, she muttered, "Until I'm seeing stars."

He frowned, suddenly noticing the scent that surrounded her. It reminded him of the fragrance of his grandmother's kitchen when she was baking. No expensive, flowery or exotically spicy perfume to conjure up lusty thoughts of satin sheets and passion-filled nights for this unusual woman. Instead she smelled like a batch of cookies!

He picked up her hand, turned it over, and lifted it to smell the inside of her wrist. "I thought I was familiar with most of the perfumes women wear, but yours is one I can't pin down."

She jerked her hand out of his grasp. "I don't imagine many of the women you know wear vanilla extract," she said dryly. She imagined he would have sleek, beautiful women on his arm . . . and in his bed. She reached behind her to untie the apron and began to blot the coffee stains on her skirt. "Look at this mess. Why didn't you watch where you were going?"

Webb was still trying to figure out why she would be wearing vanilla extract as a perfume. Instead of asking her, though, he said, "You shouldn't try to sleep and drink coffee at the same time, Betsy."

"I wasn't sleeping. I was resting my eyes."

He was intrigued by the way her eyes blazed green fire when she was challenged. "Do you usually snore when you're resting your eyes?"

Tilting her head to one side, she said haughtily, "You were never spanked enough as a child, Harry."

A short laugh escaped him. "Why Harry?"

"Why Betsy?"

"You look like Betsy Ross in that outfit. Since I don't know your real name, I have to settle for Betsy."

"Betsy sounds like someone's trusty old rifle."

"You do have a name, don't you?"

"Now, Harry," she said soothingly. "I don't think it's necessary for you to know my name. I don't—"

"My mother," he interrupted, "preferred Webb to Harry. My name is Webb Hunter."

Abby sat back in the chair, her apron balled up in her lap. "I don't need to know your name. I don't plan to sue you."

"Sue me? For what?"

"For crushing my foot and for the cleaning bill." She sighed as she fingered her skirt. "I hope this washes out. I don't have time to make another one."

Webb was silent for a minute as he digested what she said. "Don't you think you're a little old for dressing up in funny outfits?"

Just the thought of the hours it had taken to hand sew her colonial clothing made Abby's weariness come back in full force. She sighed heavily. "Definitely. At the moment I feel as ancient as this skirt is supposed to be."

Several chairs away, a small boy about three years old was fussing as he tugged on a tattered teddy bear, which an older girl was holding on to. Persistently crying "Mine" and pulling with all his might,

he finally managed to get his prized possession away
from the girl only because she let loose.

Suddenly off-balance, he began to fall, and Webb
reached over quickly to catch him. As Webb set him
on his feet, the little boy hugged his beloved teddy
bear, looking warily at Webb in case the big man
was going to have a try at taking his property.

Webb smiled down at the boy, holding his hands
out in a placating gesture. "It's all yours, kid. I don't
want it."

"What a beautiful teddy," the woman beside him
said.

Webb jerked his head around to stare at her, wondering if she had lost her mind. In his estimation,
that teddy was due for the junk heap.

Appeased, the young boy walked over to Abby,
holding out the sad-looking bear for her inspection.
Obviously, he was happy to have found at last a
kindred spirit who appreciated his cherished friend.

Realizing the honor bestowed on her, Abby carefully held the bear on her lap. "What's his name?"

"Humphrey."

Abby shook the bear's paw. "How do you do,
Humphrey?"

"What's your teddy's name?" the boy asked.

"I don't have one."

"Why?"

Smiling, Abby handed the bear back. "I guess I
wasn't as lucky as you. You take real good care of
Humphrey."

"I will. Maybe Santa will bring you a teddy if you're
good."

"Maybe."

The boy's mother called to him, and he made
Humphrey wave good-bye as he hurried back to his
chair.

Webb caught the faintly wistful look on Abby's

face. "You never had a teddy bear when you were young?" he asked.

"No," she replied simply. "Did you?"

"Several. My mother has kept them to give to her grandchildren, along with a bunch of other toys and furniture."

Her smile was sad. "That's nice."

What a strange, quixotic creature she was, Webb mused, hankering after a worn, battered bear while wearing a colonial costume and owning a sassy mouth. Sassy and kissable.

Jolted by that last thought, he returned to the subject at hand. "Don't you think a doctor should look at that foot? They may—"

He was interrupted by a voice from the doorway. The pink-uniformed volunteer was back. "'Miss Stout?" she asked, looking around hopefully.

When Abby stood up to acknowledge the summons, there was a choking sound from the man on her right.

"Stout?" Webb repeated. "Your name is Stout?"

She looked disdainfully down her nose at him, ignoring his amused smile and laughing gray eyes. "Don't say it, Harry. I've heard them all."

She might as well have been talking to herself, she thought. In fact, she was. Webb's attention had been captured by a striking blond woman who had just entered the waiting room. The woman had a distraught look on her face and seemed helplessly unsure of what to do. The newspaper tucked under her arm slipped out when she adjusted the shoulder strap of her purse. As the paper fell to the floor, several men sprang forward to assist her in her time of need, Webb Hunter gallantly joining in.

The volunteer was still waiting for Miss Stout to come forward, and Abby headed toward the door.

Each step of her left foot brought stabs of pain, but she didn't give in to the urge to favor it. Not that it would matter one way or the other. No one was looking at her. Now she knew how the guy on the beach felt when he had sand kicked in his face. The sexy blonde drew every able-bodied male to pick up those nasty, heavy sheets of newspaper, while plain old Abby was left literally to nurse her wounds.

Abby expected to be taken to Brenda, but was instead escorted to the check-in counter. The woman there needed more information regarding the payment of Brenda's bill. Since the accident was work-related, Abby put down the Historical Society as being responsible for the medical charges. She was glad the Society had insurance to cover any accidents on the property. She couldn't afford a Band-aid for a newt. She doubted if Brenda, a college student, was financially in any better position.

After the paper work was done to the clerk's satisfaction, Abby hobbled to the ladies' room. She gingerly took off her shoe, and groaned when she saw the bloodstains on her white cotton stocking. Sliding off the stocking, she examined her foot. The buckle had cut the skin, and several toes were badly bruised.

While she was washing off her foot, a nurse came in. She gave Abby's injury one expert glance, said, "You'd better let one of the doctors look at those broken toes," and disappeared into one of the stalls.

Abby stared at her toes. Broken? No wonder the darn things hurt.

She ran some water in the sink and began to rinse out her stained apron. Using soap from the dispenser, she rubbed the soiled area. After rinsing the apron, she wrung it out and found the white material free of any permanent stain.

When the nurse came back out, Abby asked, "Do you really think they're broken?"

The nurse took the wet towel from Abby and dabbed at the toes. "'Looks like it. These two here. Why aren't you in the emergency room?"

"I brought someone else in. This happened a few minutes ago in the waiting room."

The nurse threw the towel into the wastebasket. "The waiting room must be getting a little rough. What happened? Some clod step on your foot?"

Abby wouldn't go so far as to call Webb Hunter a clod. Sexy, gorgeous, virile, and disgustingly sure of himself, but not a clod. She murmured vaguely, "Something like that."

"Well, come on. I'll help you into one of the treatment rooms." Chuckling, she added, "You're the first casualty we've had from the waiting room. You deserve special treatment."

An hour later the "special treatment" had been administered to Abby's toes in the form of splints and tape and instructions to stay off her foot for several days. Abby left the hospital with Brenda, both of them bandaged and subdued by their recent encounter with the efficient emergency-room staff. Abby didn't remember until she was behind the wheel of her car that she had left her canvas bag by her chair. Her school books were in that bag. Well, she wasn't going to go back for it now. She would have to call the hospital later and hope they would hold it for her. She didn't feel like making that long walk back to the waiting room right now. Luckily she had her car keys and wallet in the pocket of her skirt.

After making sure Brenda was settled in her apartment with her leg propped up on a cushion, Abby drove home to put her own foot up for a little while until she had to get ready for work. She might not make much of an entrance tonight, but once at the piano she would be able to play for the guests in the hotel lounge, as she was hired to do. Calling in sick wasn't one of her options. Added to all her other expenses, she now had a hospital bill to pay. Taking a night off was a luxury she couldn't afford.

The canvas bag Abby had been concerned about was in good hands. Webb Hunter's hands.

All the time the bag remained on the floor by her vacant chair, Webb had expected her to return for it. By the time Turk had been treated and was ready to leave, though, she still hadn't come back. She might be irresponsible about her belongings, Webb thought, but he couldn't just leave the bag there for someone to snitch. He would leave it at the reception desk in case she ever missed her lipstick or whatever else women found necessary to carry around with them.

The bag was heavier than he had expected. Curiosity got to him, and he peeked inside. There were two thick books with several pieces of paper stuck into them. A three-ring binder full of paper was nestled between the massive tomes.

He pulled one of the books out far enough to look at the title on the spine. *Cultural and Environmental Studies of the Eighteenth Century in the Southern Colonies.* Not exactly light reading. The books were another piece of the puzzle. Was she a student?

Before Webb could examine the other title, Turk spoke gruffly from behind him. "Come on, Webb. Let's get out of here before they change their minds about letting me go."

"In a minute. I want to turn this bag in at the desk."

Shrugging, then grimacing as the movement hurt his bandaged arm, Turk said, "I'll be outside. This place smells like a hospital."

Webb plopped the bag down onto the desk near the emergency entrance, drawing the attention of a young, freckled-faced woman. Her lips parted slightly when she encountered smoky gray eyes and a smile that could melt butter. She would bet her next month's salary that this man was the type her mother had always warned her about. He had bedroom eyes. It was the first time she had actually seen them in real life.

She gulped like a stranded fish, then asked, "Can I help you?"

Webb explained how the bag had been left in the waiting room, described its owner in surprising detail, and gave her last name.

It was just her luck, the clerk thought, that he was looking for another woman. "I remember the costume," she said. "Wait a sec and I'll see what we have in our records." She immediately began typing away on the keyboard to her computer terminal, continuing even when Webb insisted the woman he was talking about wasn't a patient.

Giving him a smug smile, the clerk scanned the screen once more. "Our records show she *was* a patient in the emergency room. Abigail Stout. Treated and released."

"You must have her mixed up with the woman she brought in. They were both in colonial costume."

The clerk pushed her chair back and stood up. "Let me check."

In a few minutes she came back accompanied by the nurse who had brought Abby into the treatment room. Webb asked several questions, and the nurse calmly supplied the answers.

Webb still had the bag in his hand when he joined Turk outside.

"I thought you were going to get rid of that thing," Turk said.

"Dammit, Turk. I broke her toes."

Turk gaped at him. "Would you like to run that by me again?"

In a few terse sentences, Webb told Turk about his encounter with Abigail Stout's foot. "That's her honest-to-God name. Abigail Stout. It sounds like someone's maiden aunt."

"It's different," Turk agreed, looking down at the ground as they walked toward Webb's truck. It would be worth his life if Webb saw the grin he was valiantly but unsuccessfully trying to hold back. "So why do you still have this Abigail's bag?"

"The least I can do is return it to her personally." He yanked open the door to his truck. "I broke her toes, for Pete's sake. I don't believe it."

Turk hoisted himself awkwardly into the passenger seat with his one good hand. "She seems to have made quite an impact on you too."

"Not the way you mean. She's not my type."

"You mean she's not your usual dumb blonde?"

Webb looked over his shoulder as he backed out of the parking space. "She's not a usual anything, and definitely not a blonde. She has light rust-colored hair with streaks of gold that shine when the light hits them just right. She's got it all bunched up and tucked under some odd cap, but a few soft strands caress her face." Before he shifted into drive, Webb jerked his head around to glare at Turk. "What do you mean, my 'usual dumb blonde'?"

Grinning widely, Turk wished he had seen this

Abigail Stout, who made Webb wax lyrical about the color of her hair. Turk doubted that Webb even realized what he had said or how he had said it. "You usually date vacant blondes who haven't an original thought in their heads. But since it isn't their minds you're interested in, it doesn't really matter, does it?"

Instead of resenting Turk's blunt assessment of his taste in women, Webb stared blindly out the windshield. "I don't know what type of woman this Abigail Stout is. She dresses up like some idiotic museum piece, carries around college textbooks, and has shadows under her eyes as though she hasn't slept for a week." He hit the steering wheel with his fist. "Dammit, I hurt her."

Turk's eyes widened as he heard something in Webb's voice he had never heard before. Was "love 'em and leave 'em" Hunter actually concerned about a woman? And what did he mean by "museum piece"? Then Turk remembered the woman in colonial dress who had confronted Webb at the entrance to the emergency room. No, she wasn't Webb's usual type, and if she was Abigail Stout, this could get very interesting.

A horn honking behind them brought Webb back to what he should be doing, like driving. He pulled out of the parking lot and onto the road.

"So do you know where this Abigail Stout lives?" Turk asked practically.

"The clerk wouldn't give me the address. Said it was against hospital policy. But there can't be that many Abigail Stouts in the phone book. I'll find her."

There was no Abigail Stout in the phone directory, but Webb managed to get her address from a friend who worked for the electric company. However, she wasn't home when he rang her doorbell at six that evening. Or at seven, nine, or eleven o'clock.

He sat in his car in her driveway, wondering where she could be. Not knowing anything about her didn't help him come up with any possibilities. She could be staying with a friend, out on a date, or at a party. She could be anywhere.

Along with irritation, Webb felt a niggling concern that didn't make sense. He had only met her that afternoon. Now he was fretting about where she could possibly be and impatient to see her again, to see a woman who didn't fit any mold he tried to fit her into.

Doggone it. Where was she?

Two

The last person Abby expected on her doorstep was Webb Hunter.

The last person she wanted on her doorstep at eight o'clock on a rainy gray morning was Webb Hunter. She had managed exactly two hours and twenty minutes of sleep, and knew she looked it. She wasn't wearing any makeup, and her thick hair was piled haphazardly on the top of her head, conveniently out of the way. The comfortable old T-shirt and faded jeans she was wearing were not for public display. Her arms and shoulders were aching from the exertion of the last couple of hours over the butter churn, and perspiration had dampened her hair above her forehead.

The man's timing was lousy.

To make the occasion even more exasperating was the fact that he looked absolutely gorgeous. He was immaculately dressed in tan cords, a white shirt, and a brown leather jacket. His gray eyes were clear and bright as he looked down at her. Drops of moisture glistened on his glossy black hair, and a few dotted his jacket.

Keeping her bandaged foot out of sight behind the door, Abby asked the obvious question. "Why are you here?"

"You left this at the hospital." His leather jacket crackled softly as he held her canvas bag out to her. As soon as she had taken the bag, he raised his other hand. "I also wanted to give you this."

Her gaze was drawn to the object he was holding out to her. It was a teddy bear, a soft, fuzzy tan bear with a colonial bonnet perched on its head and a gauze bandage wrapped around one lower paw.

Webb watched her face. He had been undecided about whether or not to bring her flowers along with his apology, but he gave flowers to other women. This woman deserved something different, something as unusual and unique as she was.

Myriad emotions were reflected in her expressive green eyes, the most obvious being pure joy. Dropping the bag of books on the floor, she reached out to take the bear from him. She wouldn't have accepted flowers from him, but the teddy bear was something else again.

"Oh, she's gorgeous," she said, brightly, her smile radiant with pleasure and delight. "It is a she, isn't it?"

"Definitely," murmured Webb as the impact of her smile hit him.

"She's adorable." Cocking her head to one side, she asked, "Why did you bring me a teddy bear?"

Since it was a question he didn't have an answer for, he asked one of his own. "Why are you on your feet?"

"Well," she said reasonably, "it's darn difficult to walk to the door any other—ah! What are you doing?"

Picking her up was what he was doing.

"You," he said, "are supposed to stay off that bum foot for a few days, and I'm going to see that you do."

Her arm automatically circled his neck to hang on, her fingers gripping the supple leather covering his shoulder. She held the stuffed bear against her stomach so she wouldn't drop it.

Not knowing what one was supposed to talk about when being carried about, Abby asked, "How did you know about my foot?"

"The nurse at the hospital told me. She also said you were ordered to take it easy for a couple of days. You didn't pay much attention to her, did you? I came by last night to see how you were, and you weren't home." He didn't tell her how often he had knocked on her door. "Then this morning I saw confetti on your porch, which explains where you were last night." His voice hardened. "Even broken toes can't keep you home."

Abby could have explained about the boisterous, confetti-throwing men attending a convention at the hotel. She could have told him how many times she had been asked to play "Happy Birthday" while the confetti flew around her. She could have told him how good his arms felt around her. She could have told him all that, but she didn't. She got the impression he didn't quite approve of her, and that made her obstinate enough to withhold explanations. Besides, he seemed to feel guilty for breaking her toes, and if she told him she had been at work he might feel obligated to offer her money so she could stay home until her toes healed.

She would accept a teddy bear from him, but not charity. For seventeen years she had been forced to accept charity, and had hated it. Never again.

"If I want to go out, I'll go," she said. "You can't come into someone's house and start shoving her around."

"I'm not shoving you. I'm carrying you."

He was about to lay her down on the sofa in the living room, but she protested. "Not here. The kitchen."

"What's the matter with the sofa? If you want something from the kitchen, I'll get it."

"The butter churn is in the kitchen."

He stared down at her. "Come again?"

"My butter will be ruined if I don't get back to it." She gestured with her thumb toward the kitchen. "That way."

"Wait a minute. Why are you churning butter? They sell it in stores already made."

What a ridiculous way to hold a conversation, Abby thought. She was blatantly aware of the muscular chest against her rib cage and the arousing scent of the man holding her so close. "If you would put me down, I'd tell you."

A smile twitched at the corner of his mouth. Her chin was raised regally, as if she were about to order someone to chop off his head. "I like it this way. Now, quit stalling. Tell me why you're churning butter."

She gave him a look that would have made a lesser man drop her like a hot potato, but it didn't faze Webb. Taking a deep breath, she snapped, "I like butter." He still didn't move. "You are trying my patience, Harry. Put me down."

"The name is Webb." He didn't put her down, but he did head in the direction of the kitchen, moving easily with her held securely in his arms. Once in the kitchen, he set her down on the chair pulled up next to a wooden churn.

"My Lord," he exclaimed. "You really are churning butter."

Abby glowered at him as he stood over her. Why would she lie about a thing like that? He pulled a chair out from the table. It had a stack of books on it, and he set them on the table, noting they, too, were hefty textbooks. Then he lifted her bandaged foot and gently placed it on the chair.

When she was settled to his satisfaction, he asked, "What do you do with this"—he peered inside the churn—"glop?"

"This 'glop,' as you so elegantly put it, has to be pressed into molds. But I'll do it. I don't need your help."

She started to get up to fetch the butter molds from the counter, but a firm hand on her shoulder forced her to remain seated.

"Tell me what you need and I'll get it."

When he removed his hand, she shoved her chair back and got to her feet, only to be pushed back down again. "Abby," he said with a growl. "You are trying my patience."

"I'm not helpless."

"Maybe not, but you certainly are stubborn. This may be the only time I'll give you a chance to order me around, so you had better take advantage of it."

There was a silent battle of wills as their eyes met and held. Finally Abby gave in. He would only keep pushing her back in her chair if she kept getting up. Besides, he was bigger than she was.

Leaning back in her chair, she pointed toward the counter. "I need the wooden molds over there by the coffeepot."

"Those old wooden things?"

She smiled. Those "old wooden things" were antique butter molds lent to her by the Historical Society. They were extremely difficult to find and quite valuable. "Yes, those old things."

He brought the molds over to the table and set them in front of her. Then, without speaking, he opened several cupboards before he found what he wanted. Taking down an earthenware mug, he asked, "Do you want a cup of coffee?"

"No, thanks." She had somehow lost any say in what was going on in her own house, Abby thought as she watched him pour a cup of coffee for himself. Why was he here? She could come right out and ask him, but she wasn't sure she wanted her suspicions confirmed. If he was feeling guilty or sorry for her, she didn't want to know. She couldn't think of any other reason for his being there.

His voice broke into her thoughts. "Did the coffee stains come out of your apron?"

"Yes," she answered, surprised he remembered. "I rinsed it out right away."

"So you don't have to make another one?"

"Not yet. Hand sewing takes a great deal of time, so I was relieved that the stain came out."

"You sewed your whole outfit by hand? Why?"

"There wasn't any electric sewing machines floating around in the eighteenth century."

He conceded the point. "True, but this is the twentieth century." He paused. "Is hand sewing your outfit in the same category as wearing vanilla extract for perfume?"

"I can't very well wear Joy while dressed in an eighteenth-century costume, now, can I?"

Feeling slightly bemused, Webb said vaguely, "No, I suppose not."

She set one of the molds near the edge and began to ladle butter into it. She told herself she might as well stick to what she knew instead of treading into an area where she was bound to get lost. This man was definitely uncharted territory.

Webb leaned against the counter as he surveyed the small kitchen. Like the living room, it was spotlessly clean but sparsely furnished. There was an accumulation of numerous coats of paint on the lemon yellow cupboards, indicating years of attempts to brighten up the room. Several braided rugs were unable to cover all the worn spots on the linoleum. The small house, in an old, slightly run-down neighborhood, had looked sadly abandoned and uncared-for in the pouring rain last night as he had driven up. At first he'd thought he was at the wrong address. When he had approached the porch and seen the flaking paint on the trim around the door and windows, he'd hoped it was the wrong address. If she couldn't afford anything better, why in the world didn't she get a job?

If she did have a job, he couldn't figure out when she worked, since she had been at the hospital in the afternoon and didn't appear to be getting ready to go anywhere this morning.

Beside the books he had set on the table were several file folders stuffed with clippings and paper. The books were another piece of the puzzle that didn't fit. She apparently read history books during the day in between churning butter, for crying out loud, and went out at night. If she was in college, how did she support herself?

Like steel filings to a magnet, his eyes were drawn back to Abby. He couldn't remember ever wondering before what made a woman tick, but he wanted to know about this one. With other women, he had been more interested in the outer shell, not wanting to know what was buried inside. But there was something about Abby that bothered him, like an itch he couldn't reach to scratch.

Finally he broke the silence. "How long have you lived here?"

"A little over a year."

"Isn't it a rough neighborhood for a woman living alone?"

She slanted a look up at him. "How do you know I live alone?"

He jerked his thumb toward the sink. "There's only one cup in the sink, and you had stuff piled on the only other chair."

She looked at him a moment longer, then continued to scoop the butter out of the churn. "Very good, Sherlock."

He walked over to the table, stuck his finger into the churn, then licked it. "I'll be darned. It tastes like butter."

"I would hate to think I got the recipes mixed up and it tasted like soap."

An eyebrow raised. "You make soap too?"

She continued to press the butter firmly into a mold with the back of a spoon. "I have, but it's been awhile."

Without warning, several loud knocks sounded on the back door.

Abby received a stern look from Webb when she automatically began to get up to answer the door.

"Stay put," he ordered. "Are you expecting anyone?"

"No, but then, I wasn't expecting you either, and here you are."

He opened the door to reveal an elderly man with a yellow raincoat draped over his head. He stared at Webb. "Is Abigail here?"

Webb turned his head toward Abby, a silent question in his eyes.

"Come in, Ira," she said.

With obvious relief, Ira Burrows entered the kitchen, though he remained on the rug by the door, having been properly trained by his wife of fifty years. "There you are, Abigail. I'm sorry to interrupt while you're entertaining, but Brenda phoned to tell you she will be able to go in to work tomorrow. Her leg is much better, so she doesn't need any more time off."

Webb stood to one side, letting the man's curious gaze flow over him. He got the impression Abby didn't usually have visitors, especially men. That pleased Webb, although why it should matter to him was something he didn't care to analyze.

Abby introduced the two men to each other. "Ira is my next-door neighbor. This is Webb Hunter, Ira Burrows."

Wispy gray hair stuck out from above the older man's ears as he came out from under the raincoat and offered his hand. A broad smile crossed his lined face. "Maudie will be pleased when I tell her you're entertaining a young man. You know how she worries about you. I—"

Abby didn't give him a chance to finish. "Thanks for coming out in the rain to give me the message, Ira. I appreciate it." She hadn't wanted him to start in on her lack of a love life. He and his wife, Maudie, were dear people and good neighbors, but they occasionally became too interested in finding her a "nice young man." Having had a long and happy married life, they thought everyone else should too.

Sending Abby a sly wink, Ira opened the back door as he wrapped the raincoat over his head again. "I get it. You want to be alone. We'll see you later."

Moving rather quickly for a man of his advanced years, he was out the door and had disappeared before Abby could respond to his astonishing assessment of the situation.

She looked up to meet Webb's amused look. "Sorry about that," she said. "Ira and his wife have sort of adopted me, and sometimes get the wrong idea about things."

Webb wasn't particularly interested in Ira Burrows at the moment. "Is your phone out of order?"

"I don't have one. The Burrowses take messages if I have to be reached for anything important."

He frowned. Why didn't she have a phone? Apparently because she couldn't afford one.

Her foot was on the only other chair, but that didn't stop Webb from sitting down. Holding his coffee cup in one hand, he used his other hand to lift up her foot, then sat down on the chair and placed her foot on his thigh.

Startled, she dropped the spoon, and it clattered across the floor. He calmly bent down to pick it up and returned it to her, and then his hand settled on her bare ankle.

Abby tried to act as though it were perfectly normal for her to sit in her kitchen with her foot in a man's lap. It would have been considerably easier if her skin hadn't tingled where his hand touched it.

She cleared her throat. "So, Harry, what do you do to stay out of trouble?" she asked with forced casualness.

Hiding his amusement, Webb replied, "I build houses. And the name is Webb."

"What kind of houses?"

His hand absently stroked across the top of her foot. "Do you really want to talk about houses?"

"Why not? Oh, please, will you rinse and dry this spoon?" He did. And when he was again seated with her foot on his lap, she asked, "Don't you like houses?"

"I like to build them, but I don't necessarily find them an exciting topic of conversation when I'm with a beautiful woman."

The spoon tapped more butter into another mold with considerable force as Abby gave an unladylike snort. "So why don't we discuss houses?"

"You don't think you're beautiful?"

She looked at him skeptically. He actually sounded surprised. "One thing I learned a long time ago is to accept what can't be changed. It's called being realistic."

"Did you learn that out of those books you carry around with you?" He nodded at the books on the table. "Or those?"

"No. I learned it from a mirror." She finished the last butter mold and looked rather pleased with herself. "There," she said with satisfaction. "It looks like butter, tastes like butter. It must be butter."

"Isn't it supposed to be yellow?"

"They didn't use food coloring in the eighteenth century."

"And you have to be authentic?"

"Yup."

"You have some interesting hobbies."

"Do I?" She wished he would find someplace else to put his hand, rather than using her foot as an armrest. It made her wonder how his hand would feel touching other parts of her body. Mentally giving herself a sound shake, she asked, "Exactly which hobbies do you find interesting?"

"The lady just finished churning butter and asks me which hobbies I find interesting. You collect these sleep-inducing history books all over the place, which means you either have a hobby fooling around with colonial stuff, are taking a college course, or you have a passion for the past."

"I have a passion for eating. My hobbies, as you call them, keep this roof over my head, such as it is." She glanced up to see the puzzled look in his eyes. "I'm practicing making butter now because I'm giving a demonstration tomorrow. I like to do a run-through of anything I plan to demonstrate, to make sure it's done correctly. If I'm going to make any mistakes, I would rather make them now than in front of the tourists."

Since he still looked blank, she explained further. "The first demonstration I gave was cooking over an open hearth, and it was a complete disaster. The duck on the spit didn't get done in eight hours. The poor thing looked as pale as he was when I first put him over the fire. I couldn't get the chimney to draw properly, and the whole house was filled with smoke. Then I singed all the hair off my arms when I got the fire going too well."

He still looked bewildered. "You give colonial cooking lessons?"

Draping several lengths of cheesecloth over the molds, she replied, "That's part of what I do. As a docent at Bristol House, which means I'm a guide in period costume, I also give tours of the house and grounds." She didn't mention that she was also the assistant administrator of Bristol House, certain Webb was only making polite conversation and wasn't really interested.

"Which explains the costume you wore at the hospital yesterday, and the history books." After a brief pause, he asked, "Do you have any others?"

It was her turn to be puzzled. "Hobbies?"

"No. Passions."

Pouncing on the first thing she thought of, she said, "I have a passion for peppermint-stick ice cream. Does that count?"

"I was thinking more about the passion between a man and a woman."

"At eight o'clock in the morning?"

Lord, she was adorable, Webb thought. He had an almost irresistible urge to pull the rest of her into his lap and take her mouth with his own. She was uncomfortable with the turn the conversation had taken, but she was hanging in there. This was one woman he had to get to know better.

"It's as good a time as any," he said.

She frowned. "No offense, but you're weird."

He choked on a laugh. "Why?"

"You don't want to discuss something simple like building houses, but you choose to chat about passion with a complete stranger. Miss Manners would give you a slap on the wrist."

"I know about houses. I don't know much about you."

Abby had to give him credit for persistence. "Couldn't you start out by asking what my favorite color is?"

"What's your favorite color?"

"I don't have one."

He shook his head. "You aren't being very cooperative, Abby." Sliding back the sleeve of his jacket, he looked at his watch. "Unfortunately, I have to meet someone at a construction site in fifteen minutes. Why don't we continue this fascinating conversation later tonight, over dinner?"

The instant he took his hand off her foot, she removed it from his lap. "Sorry. I have other plans."

Shoving his chair back, Webb slowly got to his feet. His voice held a hard edge. "Another party, Abigail?"

Abby got the distinct impression the man did not like parties. She craned her head back so she could look up at him. "This is where the books on how to win friends and influence people suggest one is supposed to take no for an answer."

"I never heard of the word." Leaning down, he gripped her upper arms to lift her out of the chair, taking her weight from her foot by pressing her against his hard body.

Slowly, his lips neared hers, then softly touched hers, and she drew in her breath sharply. The gentle contact changed to a deeper, sensual kiss almost as soon as his mouth pressed against hers.

She had instinctively flattened her hands against his chest to maintain her balance, but the instant his warm mouth closed over hers, she was concerned about a different and more basic balance. The heady combination of his masculine scent and strong body overwhelmed any protest she should be making. Her insides were as churned up as the butter she had just made.

Webb's hand flowed down her back, pressing her slender frame into his lean hips and broad chest. Then he lifted his head. His hands framed her face. "I'll pick you up at seven."

"No." She wished she could have managed a more forceful reply, but she was barely able to breathe.

"Let me buy you a meal. It's the least I can do for putting your foot out of commission."

It was the wrong thing to say. It smacked of payment to ease his guilty conscience. The circumstances of her birth had forced her to accept charity as a child, but this was the first time she had been offered a charity date. She might not be able to afford much, but she owned her share of pride.

Stiffening in his arms, she said tightly, "You don't need to do penance. It was an accident."

He smiled. His fingers glided over the firm line of

her hip as he drawled, "Strange. This doesn't feel like penance. More like a reward."

She pushed against his chest, twisting away from his hand. "Go build a house, Hunter."

He let her withdraw from him, but he didn't move away. The guarded look in her eyes contrasted with her sarcastic comment, making him wonder why she was on the defensive with him. He was tempted to stay and find out, but he didn't have time.

"I'll be back," he said huskily. After another quick, hard kiss, he was gone.

Abby reached behind her to feel around for her chair. Still staring at the empty doorway he had just passed through, she sat down wearily.

She didn't need this, she thought. She really didn't need another complication in her life right now. Her dream was close to becoming a reality. Only a few more weeks and her thesis would be done. Once she was notified that her thesis had been accepted, she would be able to apply for the job her professor had said would be hers as soon as she had her master's degree.

The last obstacle, financial security, would be out of the way. When she could prove she was financially independent, she could go ahead with her plans to adopt a baby.

To have a child of her own had been her dream for a long time. Someone to give all the love stored inside her. A baby. Her child.

All her long hours and years of work were about to pay off. Nothing could get in her way. She wouldn't allow it. The years of emptiness and loneliness would come to an end when she was able to hold and cherish a small life, helping to create a loving, affectionate person who would grow from a small child to an adult. No more empty days and lonely nights. Not ever again.

Her plans didn't include kisses in the kitchen from a dark-haired man with smoky gray eyes.

Outside, Webb scowled up at the drops of water leaking through the roof of Abby's porch. Then he suddenly smiled.

Whistling under his breath he made a dash for his truck, parked at the curb in front of Abby's ramshackle house. The woman inside didn't know him well enough to realize he didn't give up when he wanted something. Right now he wanted to help her, and not because of her injured foot. He had hit upon a way, but wasn't going to tell her until it was too late.

His desire to hold her again and feel the sensual warmth of her mouth would have to wait for another time.

Three

Abby was in her bedroom when she first heard the sound of hammering. Then it stopped. It must have been her imagination, she thought. She really had to get more sleep. Now she was hearing things.

Returning to the closet, she took out another evening dress to add to the two others laid out on her bed to be dropped off at the dry cleaner's. She was royally sick of wearing the same few dresses when she worked at the hotel, but her budget wouldn't stretch to purchasing new ones.

The hanger fell from her hand when she heard pounding again. This time a man's deep laugh came between blows of a hammer. What in the world was going on? The man's voice and the drumming of the hammer sounded so close. Almost on her doorstep.

She left her bedroom to find the source of the racket. It didn't take her long. Two men were on her porch roof!

Without stopping to put on shoes, Abby stepped outside. She had removed the tape around her toes the night before so she could put on her dress shoes, and she went barefoot whenever she could, since the broken toes were still sore. She should have given her injuries longer to heal, but her employer had frowned on the slipper she had worn on one foot that first night. She couldn't afford to alienate the man who signed her paycheck.

She had to step over a pile of shingles and a large toolbox, then dodge under a ladder in order to get off the porch. The grass was still wet from the rain the day before, but that didn't stop Abby from walking out on it until she could see the two men on the roof. They were wiry and small-framed, with tanned, weathered faces. Abby put her hands on her hips and yelled up at them. "What are you guys doing up there?"

The man kneeling closest to the edge of the roof supplied the answer. "What's it look like, lady? We're fixing this roof."

"That happens to be my roof, and I didn't tell you to fix it. You have the wrong house."

Sitting back on his heels, the man reached into his pocket and withdrew a sheet of yellow paper. He read the address aloud from the paper, then looked down at her. "That's this address, isn't it?"

He had the right address. The landlord apparently had finally decided to do something about repairing the house before it fell down around her. It would have been nice if Mr. Ellison had told her ahead of time.

She raised her voice to address the man on the roof again. "Is the roof the only thing Mr. Ellison is getting fixed?"

"Who's Mr. Ellison?"

"The man who sent you here."

Folding up the paper and stuffing it back into his

pocket, the man shook his head. "Never heard of him."

It took a few seconds for Abby to digest that succinct reply. "Then who sent you?"

Picking up his hammer, the man made it clear he intended to get back to his work. "Look, lady. We have a job to do. If you have any complaints, you'll have to take them up with the boss."

"I can't very well do that if I don't know who the boss is."

He pointed with the hammer toward the truck parked out front by the curb. Considering he had answered her question sufficiently, he took a nail out of the pouch tied around his waist and began to hammer loudly.

Abby slowly walked toward the navy blue pickup. It had yellow lettering printed on the door. She read the words, then read them again when she didn't believe what she saw. Yes, she had read it right. Hunter Construction. The only person she knew named Hunter was Webb Hunter, and she had the sinking feeling Hunter Construction was Webb Hunter's business.

Her jaw set, she read the phone number underneath the title several times. Muttering the number over and over under her breath, she stormed back into the house. In short order she found her slippers and proceeded out the back door. In a minute she was knocking on the Burrowses' back door.

Maudie answered the door and greeted Abby with a friendly smile. "Hello, my dear." Opening the door wider, she invited Abby inside. "I'll put the kettle on and we can have a nice cup of tea."

"That would be lovely, Maudie, but first may I use your phone?"

"Of course. You know where it is."

Abby punched out the number she had memorized, and waited impatiently for the phone to be answered at the other end. After two rings, a woman's voice came on the line. "Hunter Construction."

"Mr. Hunter, please."

"Which one would you like to speak to?"

Abby hadn't expected there to be more than one. "How many are there?"

"There are Webb Hunter and Brad Hunter," the secretary replied patiently and with some amusement.

Abby picked the one she wanted. "Webb Hunter, please."

"I'm sorry, but he isn't here right now. Could his brother help you?"

"No, it has to be Webb." As an afterthought, Abby added, "Do you know if it was Webb Hunter who ordered his men to fix a roof on Cranston Street this morning?"

"If you'll hold a moment, I'll check the log."

Abby listened to music on the line after the secretary put her on hold. In a very short time, the woman came back. "Mr. Hunter arranged for the rush job early this morning and sent two men out immediately. Didn't they arrive?"

"They arrived, all right. Do you know how much the roofing repairs will cost?"

There was a rustling of paper; then the secretary said, "There's to be no charge."

He was probably going to mark it down as an expense for clumsiness, Abby thought. "How much does Hunter Construction usually charge for repairs such as this?" She would see he got his money, if she had to take on yet another job.

"You'll have to discuss that with Mr. Hunter. Each job has different costs, depending on the time and materials required."

"Oh, I intend to discuss it with Mr. Hunter. Will you have him call Abigail Stout at this number as soon as he can?" After reciting the number, she said, "Tell him he had better get in touch with me today or I'll personally break *his* toes."

There was a stunned silence on the other end of the line. Finally the secretary managed to speak. "I'll . . . ah, give Mr. Hunter your message, Miss . . . ah, Stout."

"Thanks." Abby hung up the phone, then glanced at Maudie. She was staring at her, gaping in astonishment.

"Good heavens, Abigail. I don't believe I've ever heard you so cross before." In her motherly fashion, she added coaxingly, "Come have a spot of tea. It will calm you."

Accepting the gentle invitation, Abby sat down at the table in the cozy kitchen. Still seething, she murmured, "The sight of Webb Hunter being strung up by his thumbs would calm me even more."

Maudie made a scolding sound as she bustled around getting cups and saucers. The ties of the bib apron she habitually wore waved back and forth as the diminutive woman went from the cookie jar, to the tea tray, to the stove for the boiling kettle. In a relatively short time there was a steaming pot of tea on the table alongside a plate containing an assortment of homemade cakes and cookies. Seeing how angry Abby was, Maudie hadn't wasted any time providing her with a panacea.

Handing Abby a cup, she asked innocently, "Why don't you let your young man take care of whatever is upsetting you?"

Reaching for one of the ginger cookies, Abby answered with a question of her own. "Which young man is that?"

"I'm referring to that nice young man Ira met yesterday." Maudie leaned forward and added sagely, "Ira said he shook hands with a firm, strong grip." She sat back in her chair, her expression making it clear she need say no more.

Apparently a strong handshake went a long way in Ira's estimation, Abby thought. "Maudie," she began hesitantly, "it's not what you think."

Maudie had selective hearing. She heard only what she wanted to hear. She didn't want to hear Abby deny an involvement with Webb Hunter, so she didn't. "He would help. Men like to help women, especially women they care about. Now, I know you're going to tell me times are different now that woman are liberated or whatever you call it, but let me tell you something I've learned about folks all these years I've been on this earth. Inside every man is a primitive desire to protect the woman in his life. It appeals to men's sense of chivalry to defend the female of the species from the dragon." Smiling, she added, "Which can be in many forms and not necessarily the fire-breathing kind."

Abby tried to visualize Webb as a knight in shining armor but couldn't. It was more satisfying to think of him strung up by his thumbs.

Maudie wasn't through yet. "Being independent is fine when there is a need for it, but between men and women who care about each other, there has to be some give and take. It wouldn't hurt you one bit to ask this young man to help if you've got a problem. It makes more sense than going around breaking people's toes or threatening to string them up by their thumbs." Giving Abby a rather naughty wink, Maudie concluded, "You can take now and give later."

Abby choked on the cookie she was eating, and began to cough. She should be used to Maudie's outrageous remarks by now, but this one had caught her off-guard.

Once she got her breath back, she tried to explain. "I don't have anyone to fight my dragons, Maudie. That man Ira met *is* the problem. He's interfering, arrogant, unpredictable, and—"

"And a handsome devil, from what Ira says."

The force went out of Abby's tirade. "Yes, he is that."

"Is he the one responsible for the little elves hammering on your roof?"

Abby laughed. First dragons, now elves. "Yes. He sent them over to pay off a debt he thinks he owes." In a few short sentences, Abby gave Maudie the details of Webb's visit to her house. Maudie already knew about Abby's injured toes. "So you see, he has to salve his conscience, and came up with the brilliant idea of having my roof mended. I know my house will never make the cover of *House Beautiful*, but he has no right to order men to work on it."

Maudie looked thoughtful. "You aren't going to be foolish and insist on paying for the work being done."

"Of course I'm going to pay for it." She grimaced, and added faintly, "Somehow."

Pursing her lips in disapproval, the older woman protested. "Abigail, be sensible. You work too hard doing all you have to do now, without taking on anything else. Only sheer grit and guts keep you going as it is."

"But *I* am doing it. That's my point. I don't want

anything given to me out of charity or guilt or whatever has motivated Webb Hunter to make this type of gesture."

Maudie nodded and said cryptically, "Your dragon."

Abby sighed. "What are you talking about, Maudie?"

"Your dragon. In your case it's your independence. It's going to take a strong man to get past that stubborn pride of yours. Webb Hunter may just be that man, if Ira is any judge of character." Maudie charged off in another direction. "So this Webb fellow is going to be phoning here?"

Abby didn't like the glint in Maudie's eyes. Hesitantly, she answered, "I left the number with his secretary."

Maudie smiled as smugly as the cat who had licked up the last of the cream. "Good," she said, then added sweetly, "Would you like another cup of tea?"

Abby imagined Maudie gleefully rubbing her hands together, looking forward to having a nice little chat with the man with the strong handshake. She knew Maudie meant well, but this was one time Abby didn't want her neighbor to interfere. Maudie and Ira had been trying to pair Abby off since she had moved next door. On the other hand, there was another way to look at it. If they thought she was involved with Webb Hunter, it might work to her advantage. They might stop nagging her about needing a man in her life and quit throwing any available male at her they could find. Later she could tell them it hadn't worked out between her and Webb.

Webb hadn't phoned back by the time Abby left the Burrowses' house. It was just as well. Hearing Maudie purr on the phone to Webb would probably prove to be more than Abby could take.

* * *

Webb got Abby's message at around ten o'clock but didn't phone her back, much to the disappointment of his secretary. His reaction to the warning tacked on to the message wasn't what she had expected either. A man shouldn't laugh when some woman threatens to break his toes.

Earlier he hadn't been sure how Abby would take his sending some men out to fix her roof. Now he knew. He might have to offer Murray and Jack hazardous-duty pay if Abby made it difficult for them to do the job. He had sent the men on impulse, with the idea of making up for hurting her, but she evidently didn't see his gesture that way. Now his brother pointed out that Abby might be offended rather than grateful. No one liked to have her shortcomings made so obvious, whether they were personal or property-related. If the house was in as poor condition as Webb had described, Abby might take exception to a stranger coming across as a do-gooder Mr. Fix-it.

Webb defended himself by stating that he had wanted to do something for the blasted woman, and getting her leaky roof repaired was the one thing he had come up with.

"Dammit, Brad," he went on. "I had to do something. I want her off my conscience. I offered to take her out to dinner, but she refused."

"Why is she on your conscience?"

"Weren't you listening? I stepped on her foot and broke her toes."

"I don't remember your having a fit of guilt when you chipped my tooth."

"I was six years old. This is different."

Brad grinned, thoroughly enjoying this. "I can see that. Why not send her flowers with a note of apology and forget her?"

"That's what I want to do, forget her. The darn woman keeps popping into my mind, and it's driving me crazy. I thought of flowers and ended up buying her a teddy bear instead. She just doesn't seem the type for flowers."

Brad choked on the cigarette he had been in the process of lighting. Gasping for air, he managed to ask, "A teddy bear? How old is she?"

"Well, she never had one as a child, so . . ." Webb's voice tapered off as his brother went into unnecessary hysterical laughter. "What's so funny?"

"Oh, Lord. I would give my favorite putter to see you go into a store and come out with a teddy bear."

"Well, get your putter out. You can come with me while I buy another one."

"You're kidding."

"Nope."

Webb rather smugly thought he had it all figured out. After Abby cooled down, he would talk to her and give her the teddy bear. She would probably be pleased he had been so thoughtful.

By the time Abby returned home from Bristol House late that afternoon, the Hunter Construction Company pickup was no longer parked in front of her house. She was so tired, she merely shrugged her shoulders and went into the house. She couldn't summon up even minor irritation at Webb or check with Maudie to see if he had returned her call. Right now she didn't care. There was a slight buzzing in her ears, and she was having difficulty focusing. This had happened to her before, and was an indication that she needed sleep badly.

It had been an unusually grueling day at Bristol House. Two guides hadn't shown up, and Brenda's injury had prevented her from taking the guests upstairs or over the extensive grounds so much of the work had fallen on Abby. Naturally it had turned out to be one of the busier days. It had also been steaming hot in the house, especially the kitchen, where she gave the butter-churning demonstration. Several guests had taken turns at the churn, but the majority of the work had been left up to Abby. Her arms and back felt the strain. Not a single breeze had come through the open leaded windows to cool the room, leaving Abby feeling like wilted lettuce.

The last of her energy was now used up washing her colonial clothing by hand and taking a quick shower. She slipped on a cool nightshirt that fell to her thighs, then collapsed on the bed after setting her alarm for seven. That would give her almost two hours' worth of sleep. Once the alarm went off, she would have time to get ready for her five-hour stint at the piano and grab a bite to eat.

She was only able to sleep for one hour. The strident peal of her doorbell jarred Abby from the depths of exhausted slumber. At first she thought it was the alarm, and batted at the switch several times, but the ringing started up again. Finally realizing it was the doorbell, she was tempted to ignore it, but whoever it was wouldn't go away. She certainly wouldn't be able to sleep through the din, and grumbling, she staggered toward the door. The person leaning on her doorbell had better have a darn good reason or have a paid-up life-insurance policy.

As soon as she opened the door and saw who it was, Abby moaned and slumped wearily against the doorjamb. "What do you want?"

Webb hadn't expected the red-carpet treatment, but he hadn't reckoned on getting her out of bed either. Taking in her mussed hair and drowsy eyes, he frowned. "Good Lord, Abby. It's only six o'clock. What in hell are you doing still in bed?" His flash of anger turned to concern. "Are you sick?"

"Yes. I'm sick of your appearing on my doorstep. Go away."

His hand blocked the door she was trying to shut in his face. This was the first time he had seen her hair hanging loose about her shoulders, and the sight had been worth waiting for. The desire to reach out and touch the silken strands was so strong, he clenched his hands into fists. As he moved to enter the house, he glanced at her feet to make sure he didn't step on her. His jaw tightened. "Why do you have the tape off your foot?"

That was it, Abby thought. The big oaf had gone too far. "It's my foot. If I want to take the tape off, I will. If I want to wear bells on each toe, I will." Warming up to a fine temper, she put her hands on her hips, unwittingly drawing attention to the fact that she had nothing on underneath the shirt. "I don't have to answer to you for anything I do, Mr. Hunter. If I want to party all night and sleep all day or run naked through the park, I will." She ignored his short laugh. "If I want to have a leaky roof, I will. And while I'm on that subject, I want to know how much I owe your company for the roof repairs."

It was a strain for Webb to keep from staring at her exquisite breasts, clearly outlined by the soft fabric. "You don't owe me anything." He had to touch her. "Kiss me and we'll call it even."

Before she could say she wouldn't, she already was. His mouth moved over hers in a slow, drugging kiss that sent spirals of need through her. She was imprisoned against him by his strong arms, and hadn't the strength to resist . . . even if she had thought of it.

Her exhaustion melted away, to be replaced by an exhilaration, a heightening of her senses, as his touch exploded over her. She leaned into him, and he took her weight, leaving his hands free to wander. A brief stroke over her hip led him to the expanse of thigh exposed by her short nightshirt.

He felt her sharply draw in her breath, felt the searing heat of his own reaction in his loins. His hands moved to her waist as he dragged his mouth from hers before he lost control. Damn, she felt good. She felt good, tasted good, and he wanted to experience more of her. But this was not the time to give in to the desire raging through his bloodstream.

"Abby," he murmured huskily. "Look in my jacket pocket."

Abby brought her arms down from around his neck. She hadn't the faintest idea how they had gotten there in the first place. Dazed, she trailed her hand down the smooth surface of his jacket to one of the pockets, but felt nothing.

His intent gaze never left her face. "The other one."

This time she found a small furry object and withdrew it. It was another teddy bear. With a faint smile, she looked up at him. "Don't you think it's a little strange for a grown man to walk around with a stuffed bear in his pocket?"

"I've been doing a lot of strange things lately."

Giving in to the appeal of her creamy skin, he brushed her throat with light, butterfly kisses. "Have dinner with me tonight, Abby."

Closing her eyes against the compelling need, she pushed herself away from him, fighting the temptation to accept his invitation, fighting the desire his masculinity offered. "I can't. I have other plans."

He didn't like her answer, but he accepted it. "Tomorrow night?"

She shook her head.

"You give me a time you will be available, then."

Again she shook her head, unable to explain why she refused to go out with him. There were so many reasons all jumbled together in her mind, too complicated to define in a few words. Her dragon was rearing its ugly head again. She was so accustomed to keeping her thoughts and feelings to herself, it was impossible to put them into words now. She wasn't used to having to explain herself to anyone.

"Now is not the time to lose your voice, Abby. Are you involved with someone else? Is that the problem? I would rather know now than later."

She was about to shake her head again, but stopped. That was taking the coward's way out. "It's . . . I have my life planned out very carefully. I don't have time for dinner dates, nor do I want any."

"You have time for going to confetti-throwing parties but not enough time to have dinner with me? Your plans don't make allowances for eating?"

Rubbing her forehead wearily, she said in a low voice, "Just take no for an answer, Webb. Please. I'm too tired to argue with you."

The use of his name surprised and pleased him, even though her voice trembled slightly from exhaustion when she said it. There were dark shadows under her eyes, and she was holding her body stiffly, as if it were a strain just to stand up. Making a tactical retreat, he didn't press her further to go out to dinner. He did wonder, for about the hundredth time, why he kept coming back for more rejection. He had to be nuts.

"All right, Abby. You win. I'll go." At the door, he

turned to look back at her. After a long moment, he finally said, "Take care of yourself."

Abby should have been relieved he had left so easily. Wasn't that what she wanted? Then why did her house suddenly feel so empty? Why did she feel so empty? It was because she was tired. That had to be it.

As she returned to her bedroom to begin dressing for work, a frown creased her brow. She had to be mistaken if she thought he looked hurt when he left her house. It must have been her imagination. There had been something in his eyes when he had paused at the door to look back at her, but she found it hard to believe he was in any way affected by her refusal.

She had enough on her mind without worrying about Webb Hunter's feelings. A man like him could have any woman he wanted. It was inconceivable that he was disappointed because he couldn't have her. She sighed. He was the nearest thing to her vision of a knight in shining armor, but her dragons were powerful and possessive. Darn Maudie for bringing up dragons.

She had sent the knight away out of fear. He had accidentally broken her toes. If she let him, he could break her heart.

For most of the evening every table was occupied in the hotel lounge, as were the stools around the bar. A wedding reception was taking place in one of the ballrooms, but many of the guests had overflowed into the lounge. Abby figured either the ballroom was too crowded or the champagne had gone flat.

The hotel catered to a moneyed clientele who were not the type to get rowdy. One of the reasons Abby had taken this job was the fine reputation the hotel had in the community. She had previously worked in places that were little better than dives. Here she didn't have to fight off men who had too many hands and too much to drink.

Playing the piano had been a way of earning money in the evenings while she attended college, and she had been thankful many times for the patient woman who had given her piano lessons in exchange for babysitting. The woman had been a disciplined teacher, insisting on hours of practice from her student. Fortunately, the foster family Abby had been living with then had a piano, and her foster parents hadn't minded her using it. Abby hadn't realized at the time how she would be putting her skill to practical use.

She gazed around at the well-dressed crowd as she played a standard tune. Several faces were familiar, regular guests who stayed at the hotel while on business. She spotted an elderly couple holding hands like the newlyweds they had been fifty years ago. An hour earlier she had played "The Anniversary Waltz," and they had danced alone on the small dance floor while their friends gathered to watch.

Her gaze skimmed lightly around the room, passing over the entrance as a couple came in—then she jerked her attention back to the couple. Her fingers faltered for several beats, until she recovered from the shock of seeing Webb stroll in with a stunning blonde on his arm. It hadn't taken him long to find a substitute dinner partner, she thought bitterly.

The small lamp hanging over her music was the only light in the corner of the lounge where her piano was. It was doubtful he would recognize her in the dimness, even if he managed to tear his gaze away from the woman at his side.

Webb was pulling a chair out from a recently vacated table to seat his lady friend, who was smiling coyly at him. How the woman could sit down in that tight slinky dress without splitting a seam was, Abby figured, a credit to the clothing manufacturers.

They were a striking couple: Webb's charcoal suit, ebony hair, and tanned features a high contrast to his blonde companion's porcelain complexion and sparkling white dress. The woman fit Abby's impression of the type Webb would be attracted to, rather than a plain Jane like herself.

It hurt. It honestly hurt to see Webb with another woman, an exceptionally beautiful woman. The extent of that hurt was deeper than Abby expected, had asked for, or wanted.

One of the waiters brought her a slip of paper with a song request on it, and she pulled herself back to her work. Priding herself on being a realist, she accepted the way things were. Men like Webb went for women like the sophisticated blonde. Abby didn't necessarily have to like it, but she had to accept it.

During the next hour, she continued playing background music that blended with the clatter of glasses and the low mumble of conversation. She didn't look in the direction of Webb's table again.

Webb was bored. Whatever had possessed him to call Carla? he wondered. Possessed. That was exactly how he felt about the woman who kept flooding his thoughts, even when he was with someone as sexually provocative as Carla. If he had hoped to exorcise Abby by spending the evening with another woman, it wasn't working. Carla's seductive glances and superb figure left him cold . . . which scared the hell out of him.

While Carla related the details of her latest trip to Palm Springs, Webb's gaze trailed around the room, eventually settling on a waiter who was heading toward the corner of the lounge where the grand piano stood. He saw the waiter hand a piece of paper to the woman seated at the piano. As the pianist leaned forward to accept the paper, her features were illuminated by the small lamp hanging above the piano.

His body stiffened and his eyes narrowed as he stared at the woman. She was wearing a shimmering black dress and her hair was drawn to the back of her head in a sophisticated coil. He had either lost what was left of his mind or the woman behind the piano was Miss Abigail Stout.

He had the absurd notion of going over to the piano and demanding an explanation. Why hadn't she told him she had to work tonight when she had refused his invitation to dinner? He would find out later. After he calmed down, after he figured out why he was so damn angry.

Abby began to move her fingers over the ivory keys to play "You Light Up My Life" for a young couple who considered the tune "their" song. Requests were heavier tonight than usual, but Abby didn't mind honoring them. It was an indication someone was listening to her music, and the requests were a change from her usual choice of tunes.

The waiter approached the piano again. "We have to stop meeting like this, Abby," he said.

She grinned. "Maybe you can talk Ferris into installing a jukebox. Save you trips across the lounge. Of course, then I'd be out of a job."

"He'd never go for it. I think I'd rather put in for permission to wear tennis shoes." He handed her a piece of paper. "Another little something from your fans. You'll love this one."

"Not 'The Anniversary Waltz' again?"

"Not even close." Chuckling, he returned to his duties.

Abby unfolded the paper and read, "Please play 'The Teddy Bear's Picnic.' " Slowly raising her head, she looked in the direction of Webb's table, but he was engrossed in the blonde. It *could* be a coincidence, she thought. A strange coincidence, considering Webb's penchant for teddy bears and his presence in the lounge.

Webb and his companion left shortly after Abby finished playing the teddy-bear tune. She saw them leave, and didn't want to speculate on where they were going or what they would be doing. She told herself she didn't care. The thing to do was to forget Webb Hunter. He seemed to have found it easy enough to forget her.

By the time the lounge closed, at two in the morning, Abby was feeling oddly detached. She walked to her car on automatic pilot and started it in a fog of exhaustion. She had driven out of the parking lot before she realized she hadn't turned her lights on. Rolling down her window, she let the cool night air blow across her face to revive her before she had an accident.

About halfway home, she heard a loud, blunt noise, and the steering wheel was almost pulled out of her hands as the car jerked sideways. Having experienced this last month, Abby knew what had happened. She had a flat tire.

Webb was driving back toward the hotel after spending two hours restlessly pacing around his home. He had dropped a pouting Carla off shortly after leaving the hotel, and had found it impossible to relax once he was home. He knew he wouldn't be able to sleep if he went to bed, so he had made himself a drink and changed into a comfortable pair of faded jeans and a sweater.

Finally, at about one-thirty in the morning, he had given in to the inevitable. He had to see Abby. As he neared the hotel he slowed down when he saw a car pulled to the side of the road. A woman in a black evening gown was trying to jack up the car. He smiled grimly as he recognized the motorist.

He was going to get a chance to chat with Miss Abigail Stout sooner than he had expected.

Four

Abby had been aware of the car slowing down as it approached. She sighed with relief as it passed her; then her heart lurched with fear when she saw it make a U-turn and pull up behind her. Tightening her grip on the jack she had been using to raise the car, she slowly straightened to face the shadowy figure emerging from the strange car.

The driver had left his headlights on. They illuminated her and her car, but made it impossible for her to see the features of the silhouetted man coming toward her. Her fingers curled more tightly around the cold steel, her body poised in readiness for whatever threat this man presented.

A deep voice cut through the dark curtain of night. "You won't need the crow bar, Abby. I'm not in the mood to ravish your body or steal your hubcaps right now. Maybe later."

Abby slumped against her car in relief, recognizing the voice. Letting the jack handle fall to the pavement with a clang, she flexed her hand several times to get the circulation flowing again. Webb might not sound very happy to see her, but she was delighted to see him. She watched as he stepped into the light, and saw that he had changed clothes and was furious. Perhaps his evening with the lady in white hadn't been a successful one. It didn't occur to her that she was the cause of his fury.

She gulped nervously. "I didn't recognize the car. You usually drive a truck."

He stood in front of her, his hands on his hips, his legs slightly apart, as he glared down at her. "Why discuss what I drive when you could be explaining what in hell you think you're doing out here alone?"

The proprietary tone of his voice made her stare in astonishment. He had just been out with another woman, for crying out loud, and now was acting as if he had a right to know where she was and what she was doing. She wasn't experienced enough with the vagaries of a man's mind to realize his anger was his way of dealing with his fear for her safety.

The surge of adrenaline she had experienced at the hint of danger had drained her already exhausted body. She just wanted to go home. "How do you feel about changing a flat tire?" she asked.

"Ecstatic."

Bending down, he retrieved the jack handle and finished jacking up the car. After removing the tire, he pulled the spare out of the trunk. When he dropped it onto the pavement and heard a sickening thud, he realized it wasn't in any better shape than the other tire.

The piercing look he sent Abby spoke volumes. He returned the spare to the trunk, along with the other tire. After slamming down the trunk, he extended his hand toward her, palm up.

"Your keys," he said.

"Why do you want them?"

"To lock the trunk and the doors. You're coming with me."

"I can't just leave my car by the side of the road."

"Sure, you can, Abby. You can do a lot of things. You can churn butter, go to work with broken toes, and drive me bananas. Give me your keys or lock your car yourself. Either way, your car stays here and you are coming with me."

Her hand was shaking as she took the key out of the ignition and locked the door. Now that she knew she was safe, a reaction was setting in. The keys jangled against the door until Webb removed her hand and finished the job.

Pocketing her keys, he turned her around and enfolded her in his arms, muttering under his breath. He was experiencing a few violent reactions of his own as he tried not to think of the horrible things that could have happened to her. The late hour, her tantalizing dress, the deserted stretch of road . . . He held her tighter to absorb the shudders in her body, wanting to protect her from life's harsh realities at least for a little while.

As her body became still, he drew his hands down her arms, allowing space between them so he could see her face. There was a huskiness in his voice as he asked, "Are you all right?"

She took a deep breath. "Yes. I'm fine."

"Of course you are," he said roughly. "That white face is only a figment of my overactive imagination." A muscle clenched in his jaw, and his fingers tightened almost painfully around her arms. "I hope you were scared silly, Abby. Remembering how you felt before you knew it was me might make you more careful when you're roaming the streets in the middle of the night."

"You make it sound as though it were my fault the tire blew. I don't go out of my way to get flat tires."

"You don't go out of your way to make sure your spare tire is in good condition, either."

"I had to use the spare a couple of weeks ago when another tire blew. I forgot that I haven't had a chance to get it fixed."

He stared down at her as a mixture of emotions crossed his face. Disbelief, amazement, anger, and consternation fought with one another. Anger won.

"You need a keeper, Abby. You really do. How you've survived this long without one is a miracle."

"No, thanks. I've had a handful of keepers. I prefer to be on my own."

Webb thought she was referring to men, and found the idea of her with other men an unpleasant one. Unpleasant was too tame a word. He hated it.

His mouth was set in a grim line as he led her back to his car and deposited her in the passenger seat. "Not another word out of you, Abby, until we get to your house."

The drive to her house was accomplished in complete silence. Once there, Webb followed her inside without being invited, but Abby wasn't about to quibble over that minor infraction of etiquette. It would be like poking a sleeping tiger. For all Webb's kindness toward her back there on the road, she was aware of the fury still emanating from him.

Wearily, she sat down on the couch and leaned her head back, unaware of the heat in his eyes as he gazed at her. Her slender form was emphasized by the tight black dress, and an expanse of shapely leg was exposed by the slit in the side of the dress as she kicked off her high-heeled shoes and crossed one leg over the other. Webb purposely stayed several feet away from her, wanting to maintain his anger so the desire to touch her wouldn't take over. He watched her lean forward to rub her injured foot.

"Do your toes still bother you?" he asked.

She shook her head. "Not much. They are a little sore from the shoes I have to wear to work." She paused. "I want to thank you for stopping tonight. It would have been a long walk home."

"What if it hadn't been me? What would you have done? Used the jack on whoever decided to take advantage of the opportunity you were presenting?"

"Probably. I have great survival instincts."

"Really? Are those the same instincts you used when you hiked your dress up over your thighs while you were kneeling by the car earlier?"

If Abby had had the energy, she would have taken exception to that remark. "I do what I have to do," she murmured, "when I have to do it. If that means I have to change a tire at two-thirty in the morning in an evening gown, then that's what I do."

"And one of the things you have to do is play the piano every night at that hotel?"

"Yes." So he *had* seen her. She still hadn't been sure.

"Is there any particular reason why you couldn't tell me you had to work when I asked you to have dinner with me? I wouldn't have been shocked. Most of the people I know work. I work. Why couldn't you tell me?"

"Since it was going to be a token date, I didn't think my refusal required an explanation." She quickly covered the yawn that escaped.

Webb resumed the stance Abby was becoming familiar with every time he was angry—legs spread apart, hands on hips. "I asked you out because I wanted to see you again. Why do you call it a token date?"

"You felt guilty because you stepped on my foot and broke my toes. The dinner invitation was a way of easing your conscience." Her explanation sounded a little lame at best, but it was the only one she had. "I don't go out on charity dates."

He took a steadying breath to cool his flash of temper. Getting mad at her wasn't going to give him the answers he needed. "Abby," he said slowly. "Are there other crazy people in your family, or are you the only one?"

She was so tired, she didn't think before she spoke, and she gave away a piece of her past she hadn't intended to reveal. "Could be. I wouldn't know."

His anger completely disappeared as the meaning of her quietly spoken words sunk in. After a thoughtful pause, he walked over to the couch and sat down beside her, his hard thigh brushing hers. "You have no family at all?"

She shifted over on the cushion in an attempt to move away from him. "Not that I know of. If there are any loonies floating around, you head the list. Why don't you go home?"

His arm slipped around her waist, and he dragged her back against him, alarmed at how slight her weight was. Damn her foolishness. She didn't eat enough, sleep enough. He should let her get some rest now, but he wouldn't be able to sleep himself unless he got some answers.

He countered her question with one of his own. "Why don't you relax? Close your eyes if you want, but talk to me."

Her green eyes met his warily. "What happened to the fire-breathing man who was having such a good time yelling at me?"

"There's something you need to know about me, Abby. I don't stay mad long."

Her spine stiffened as his fingers began to massage her tense back. "There's something you had better know about me. I *do* stay mad."

His other hand came up to touch her pale cheek. "Abby, I was scared out of ten valuable years of my life when I saw you alone on that dark road. I had R-rated visions of all sorts of nasty things that could have happened to you if I hadn't spotted you when I did. You got off lightly with a tongue-lashing, considering how I felt. You could have suffered a lot worse if some other man had come by who didn't possess my finer qualities."

Abby was thankful he dropped his hand away from her face, especially when she had been tempted to nuzzle her cheek against his warm palm. "Why would a man of such fine qualities be out cruising the streets at that hour of the morning?"

"I was coming back to the hotel to see you," he said simply.

"I didn't think you knew I was there."

"Oh, I knew. I even requested a tune."

" 'The Teddy Bear's Picnic'?"

He nodded. "I've always considered myself a relatively smart man, but I couldn't figure out why you hadn't told me you had to work when I asked you out. I had to come back to find out."

She wished he would just leave. On top of everything else she had to do tomorrow, she had to arrange for someone to tow her car and fix her tire. After a couple of hours of sleep, she would be able to cope better with everything, including Webb.

"Well," she said wearily. "Now you know."

"Only that you work at the hotel, guide people around Bristol House, and have no family. Instead of giving me enough to solve the puzzle, you grudgingly add more pieces." He pulled out her hairpins, releasing the glorious mass of soft curls from their confinement. Gently combing his fingers through the strands, he added, "You aren't exactly overly generous with information about yourself, Abby."

"It's because of my dragon," she said, in a muffled, sleepy voice. She slumped against him, giving in to the exhaustion seeping into her bones and to the delicious, soothing stroking of his fingers in her hair. It felt wonderful to be able to lean on someone else for a change, if only briefly. Not just anyone, though. Webb Hunter. Sighing heavily, she closed her eyes as her head nestled against his shoulder.

His arms closed around her. "Your dragon?"

"Mmmm. That's what Maudie calls it. Several of my foster parents called it being stubborn. I call it being independent."

Her breathing was beginning to deepen, and Webb realized she was falling asleep. He smiled to himself. He had pictured her falling asleep in his arms, although not exactly this way. But it was enough just to hold her for now.

Stretching his legs out onto the cushions, he leaned his head back against the throw pillows, cradling Abby securely between his body and the back of the couch. His eyes closed as his fingers wove through her hair. He would be able to sleep now. Some of the missing pieces had fallen into place. Not all of them, but he could wait for the rest. One important piece was the last thing he thought of before he slept. The "handful of keepers" she had mentioned had been foster parents, not other men.

Abby's internal clock roused her a few minutes before seven. For some reason her mattress felt exceptionally lumpy this morning. She moved her head to find a more comfortable position on the pillow. Silly darn thing seemed to have a life of its own. It was moving up and down under her cheek.

Her eyes flew open. Pillows didn't have lives of their own, but the chest she was lying on did. She let out a startled scream.

Calm gray eyes stared back at her as she tried to scramble off Webb, but her dress was caught between his legs. "Good morning," he murmured softly.

Tugging at her dress, she asked breathlessly, "What are you doing here?"

"Recovering from a heart attack. Why did you scream? I know I need a shave, but I can't look that bad."

"I . . . you . . . we . . ." she stammered.

He chuckled at her confusion. "I . . . you . . . we fell asleep. Nothing to get hyper about." His arm snaked out to grab her, pulling her back down on his chest. "You went to sleep without giving me a good-night kiss."

"It's morning," she said abstractedly.

"I'll take a good-morning kiss later."

His voice held a hint of amusement, but there was no humor evident as he brought her mouth down to his. There was a raw hunger and sensual demand as he immediately coaxed her lips apart to enable him to feast upon her warmth.

Abby's fingers clenched his hard shoulders as tremors skimmed along her flesh when his mouth shifted to make a more intimate claim. A soft sound of yearning vibrated deep in her throat, and he rolled her body hard against his.

The heated impact of her slender length took his breath away, and his hands moved down her spine to her hips to control her restless movements. The soft kiss hadn't turned out to be as casual as he had intended. A few more moments and he wouldn't be able to stop. Reluctantly, he released her.

His breath brushed across her throbbing lips as he spoke. "If that was the good-night kiss, I think we better skip the good-morning one," he said huskily.

He skimmed a warm finger across her mouth, then gently lifted her by the waist so that they were sitting side by side. He reached over to adjust her skirt where it had fallen open, seductively exposing her thigh. "Don't tempt me," he said. "I don't have a lot of willpower until I've had my first cup of coffee."

Abby smiled faintly. It would take more than a cup of coffee to quell the rioting sensations in her body, but if he could treat the kiss lightly, so could she. "Two cups of willpower coming up," she said as she stood up and headed toward the kitchen.

After measuring the coffee grounds and water, she plugged in the coffee maker. She wondered if she should offer to fix him breakfast. The rules of behavior taught to her by her foster parents had never included how to treat a man who had spent the night.

She peered into the refrigerator. It didn't take long to inventory the contents. One egg and a container of blueberry yogurt did not a breakfast make. She had planned to go to the grocery store after receiving her paycheck from the hotel tomorrow, but that wasn't any help now.

She suddenly heard running water, and quickly shut the refrigerator door. A deep baritone voice singing snatches of a pop tune came through the thin walls. Webb was taking a shower.

Damn, she felt so inadequate. He was taking it all

in stride, but she hadn't ever had a man spend the night with her before. She frowned as she retrieved the egg from the refrigerator and cracked it into a shallow bowl. Apparently this was common stuff for Webb. She beat the egg with a fork, adding some cinnamon and nutmeg. Well, she would feed him and send him on his way. If it wasn't what he was used to, that was just too bad.

She dipped two slices of bread in the egg mixture, fried them, and then placed them on a plate, covering them to keep them warm. Honey would have to do for syrup. She was out of that, as well as butter.

She was pouring the coffee when Webb sauntered into the kitchen, a towel hanging around his neck, barely covering his naked muscular chest. His black hair was still damp, and he had shaved off the dark stubble that had shadowed his face. He certainly had made himself at home. She wondered if this was his normal behavior after spending the night with a woman.

She watched him slip his arms into his shirt, thinking it was a shame to cover up such a magnificent example of the male physique. A corner of his mouth curved up as he acknowledged her stare, clearly enjoying her interest.

"Something smells good," he said.

"Sit down and eat while it's hot. I'm going to change my clothes."

"Aren't you going to join me?"

She shook her head, then lied. "I'm not hungry. Oh, if you have to leave before I get back, thanks again for driving me home."

His gaze held hers briefly, and he wasn't surprised when she looked away. His attention shifted to the table, where a single plate was set at one end. His gray eyes darkened with suspicion, but before he could protest, Abby had left the kitchen.

He opened the refrigerator door and looked inside. He didn't like what he saw.

Abby turned off the hot water and let the cold water run for a few minutes, hoping it would jolt her awake. She had another day to get through. It had started with a pip of a complication in the form of Webb Hunter, but he would be gone by the time she was dressed. After all, he had a business to run. He had done his good deed for the day in rescuing her. There was no reason for him to stay any longer.

But Webb was seated at the table when she returned to the kitchen. His empty plate was in the sink. In front of him a large Royal Albert platter with a familiar pattern of red and yellow roses around the rim. A fragrant assortment of coffee cake, homemade rolls, and doughnuts sat on the platter. Abby assumed Maudie had seen the strange car in her driveway and accurately guessed whose it was.

Webb was munching away on a cinnamon roll, and his gaze wandered over her tan slacks and peach blouse. He frowned slightly when he saw her glossy hair was confined by a ribbon at the nape of her neck, then realized she was staring at the platter.

He gestured toward it with his cinnamon roll. "A sweet little old lady pounded on the back door while you were taking a shower. She shoved the platter at me, winked, gave me a thumbs-up signal, and left." He got up and pulled out the other chair. "Sit. I'll get you a cup of coffee."

Along with the coffee, Webb brought her a plate and piled several rolls on it. "Am I correct in assuming that lady was the other half of the elderly man who came to the door the other day?"

Eyeing the tempting rolls in front of her, Abby nodded. "Her name is Maudie."

"The same Maudie who talks about dragons?"

Abby blinked. "How did you know that?" Oh, lord, she thought. Maudie wouldn't have told Webb he had been chosen to be the slayer of her dragons, would she? Darn right she would.

Helping himself to another roll, Webb answered her question. "You did. Last night."

"I did?"

"You were half-asleep at the time. Have one of these. They're delicious. I'll make a few phone calls about your car when I get to my office. It'll get four new tires and a general going over. You should have it back tomorrow if they can get right to it. If you need to go anywhere, today, I'll take you."

Abby dropped onto her plate the roll she had picked up. "You have no right to take over my car repairs. I can't—"

"Don't tell me you can't afford it. I already know that. I'm paying for the repairs, and you can pay me back when you're able. If it helps that prickly independence of yours, I'm doing if for me, not you. I wouldn't be able to sleep nights, wondering if that old car had broken down somewhere, leaving you stranded."

Abby swallowed with difficulty, fighting the absurd feeling that she was about to start bawling. She could take his ranting and raving more easily than she could take his kindness.

Webb watched her closely. Dammit, he thought. He had as much finesse as a pile driver. He didn't regret what he had said, but he did wish he had been a bit more tactful about it. "Abby," he began, "I—"

This time she interrupted him. She cleared her

throat and lifted her chin. "I'm due at Bristol House this afternoon, but I can get a ride with Brenda. I'm scheduled to work at the hotel tonight from nine until two, but I'll call one of the waiters. I wouldn't ask you to stay up that late just to taxi me around."

"You didn't ask. I'm offering. We'll compromise. You arrange for a ride to Bristol House and I'll take you to the hotel tonight."

Thinking of the lady in white, Abby said, "If you have other plans, don't change them in order to chauffeur me around."

She was attempting to put him off, but he wouldn't allow it. "I have no other plans." He pushed her plate closer to her. "I know you said you aren't hungry, but at least eat one roll."

Ignoring his request, she sat back in her chair. "I haven't had anyone boss me around this much since I was seventeen."

"What did you do about it then?"

"I left."

"What are you going to do about it now?"

She paused. "I haven't decided." She took a bite out of the roll, not really tasting it. "I'm eating this because I want it, not because you told me to."

"Right." At least she was eating something. "I don't suppose this would be the right time to ask you to have dinner with me before you have to go to work tonight."

She shook her head. She wasn't used to someone else being in control, and had to take a stand somewhere. "I'll be ready at eight-thirty."

With Abby, Webb knew he had to accept defeat along with a few victories. "I'll be here."

He not only drove her to work that night, but stayed the whole five hours she was at the piano. During one of her breaks, he had sandwiches and a big glass of milk waiting for her. A small white teddy bear kept her company from a corner of the keyboard, where Webb had placed him when she first sat down to play.

Her hints about his being bored or tired went unheeded. He stayed.

On the way home, he stopped at an all-night coffee shop and ordered a cup of coffee for him, a glass of milk for her, and two pieces of apple pie with double scoops of vanilla ice cream on top.

Later, as he walked her to her door, she stumbled sleepily up the porch stairs and leaned against the wall while he unlocked the door.

He pushed it open and flicked on the hall light. "In you go, Sleeping Beauty."

"Roll me in. I can hardly move. I ate too much. If I can't make it through the doorway, it's all your fault."

He touched her cheek with one finger, gently stroking her soft, downy skin. "It was my pleasure. Come out with me tomorrow night, Abby. Give me pleasure again."

"It gives you pleasure to watch me eat?" she asked, her eyes laughing at him.

"Among other things." His fingers went under her chin to tilt her face up. His head lowered and his mouth opened over hers.

Abby's heart seemed to stop beating, then raced madly. His touch, his scent, his warmth drew her closer, made her want to get even closer. Her hands went to his shoulders and around his neck as her lips parted to welcome his thrusting tongue, meeting and caressing it with her own.

Her passionate response shocked him . . . and aroused him unbearably. His hand caressed her throat and her pulse beat like a mad thing against his fingers. His mouth broke away from hers to follow the path of his hand, down her neck to the satiny skin below. His fingers sought the buttons of her blouse, loosening two before he stopped.

"'Lord, what am I doing?" He buried his face in her neck, crushing her in his powerful arms. He held her for a minute in silence, then lifted his head to look at her. "I promised myself I wouldn't do this."

Abby began to ask why, but before she could speak he claimed her mouth once again. She felt a restraint in him. His shoulders were taut under her hands, and he kissed her with a desperate male hunger that was in conflict with the rigidness of his body.

Abruptly he jerked his mouth away from hers, and his eyes were smoldering as he looked down at her. "So much for my noble promises," he murmured in self-disgust. "You should be stopping me, since I don't seem to be able to stop myself."

She gazed up at him with bewilderment. "Why?" she breathed.

"Abby." He sighed heavily. "Have you ever been with a man before?"

She stiffened. "Have you ever been with a woman before?"

"I'm thirty-five, for Pete's sake," he snapped angrily.

"I'm twenty-five."

"That's no answer, dammit."

"Yes, it is."

For a long moment he stared at her, knowing he could have her tonight, knowing his body was aching for her, knowing it wasn't the right time.

With his hands at her waist, he gently pushed her through the doorway. "Good night, Abby."

"Good . . . night," she murmured in confusion to the empty hall.

She had just had a trip to ecstasy and somehow had been detoured. Somewhere along the line she had misread the signs, or wasn't experienced enough to interpret them correctly.

What in the world was she going to do about Webb? She should be concentrating on her thesis, not on him. She needed to remember what she was working for instead of wanting to be with him.

Five

About twenty people, including several children, were standing at a respectful distance from Abby as she demonstrated candle-making in the large kitchen at Bristol House.

A huge kettle was hanging from a hook over a fire laid in the vast fireplace. Near one wall two poles were laid across the backs of two chairs. Dipped candles would be hung on these to cool.

Abby was holding a wooden rod with six wicks attached to it. They were dangling down. "The wicks were made of spun hemp, cotton, or milkweed," she told the group. "They were twisted and doubled, with the loop slipped over the rod. Then the wicks were twisted again for additional strength."

She slowly dipped the wicks into the kettle, which contained melted tallow, then slowly lifted them back out. "The candles must be allowed to cool and harden between dippings. If they cool too fast, they will often crack or become brittle. To make a candle approximately one inch in diameter takes many dippings."

She set the rod across the two poles, then picked up the next rod of wicks and returned to the kettle to repeat the process.

One of the women in the group asked shyly, "Why are the candles green? Shouldn't they be white?"

Abby smiled. "We try to be as authentic as possible, but finding bear grease or deer suet in this day and age isn't as easy as using a tallow made from bayberry."

"The bayberry tallow smells much better, too," added Marilyn, who was assisting Abby.

There were a few amused chuckles from the group.

Abby went on. "The berries were gathered in late autumn and melted down in boiling water. The fat from the berries was skimmed off, and that fat forms the tallow. When we want to make candles, we melt the tallow again any time we want, instead of having to wait until late September to pick the berries."

Abby was unaware that another person was listening from a position by the back door. Webb was standing behind her, only able to see her back when the people in front of him moved, but he could hear her continuing her explanation as she walked back and forth between the chairs and the kettle.

"Every ounce of fat was saved from cooking in order to preserve as much grease as possible for candle-making. You may have noticed the planks on the floor under the rack holding the candles. They catch the occasional drop of tallow, which was collected to be melted down again."

"How often did the women have to make candles?" asked a man holding a small child in his arms.

"Usually a winter's supply would be made in the fall. On a good day, an average of two hundred candles could be made. A lot depended on the weather, how many other chores the woman of the house had to do, how many children she had to help her. The household would use the candles sparingly, rising at first light and going to bed when the sun had set." She smiled at the man who had asked the question, holding a rod of wicks out to him. "Would you like to have a go at making candles?"

The man backed away. "No, thanks."

When the man stepped back, Abby saw Webb by the door. He met her startled glance with a lazy smile and a brief nod. She paused for only a fraction of a second. What in the world was he doing here? Turning to the man's wife, she spoke in a stage whisper loud enough for everyone to hear. "Some things don't change. Men didn't help in the eighteenth century either."

The women laughed more spontaneously than the men, and Abby glanced at Webb, catching his slow, amused smile.

Turning back to the group, she announced, "Dipped candles similar to the ones we have been making this afternoon are available for sale in the gift shop, which just happens to be the last building we will show you."

She moved toward a door that led to an inner room. "The next room you will be seeing is what we would call the living room today."

Slowly the kitchen began to clear of people, except for Marilyn and Webb. Marilyn latched on to him, smiling charmingly as she pointed to the rack of hanging candles, and began to explain the procedure in case he had missed any part of the demonstration.

With one last glance at Webb, Abby followed the group into the other room. Apparently Webb preferred a private tour.

An hour later Abby was walking back toward the house after turning the group over to Brenda, who would show them the herb garden, the well house, and the family graveyard.

Webb was sitting on a rustic bench outside the house, and he watched her stroll through the unmown grass, her long, full skirt swaying as she walked. A slight breeze ruffled the puffy sleeves of her shift and tossed her long white apron in waves over her skirt. She looked as though she had just stepped out of an eighteenth-century painting. Absorbed in the picture she made, Webb felt transported to an age when life had been more primitive.

He was feeling a bit primitive himself right now. The friendly guide had furnished him with a few more interesting tidbits about Miss Abigail Stout, tidbits Abby had neglected to share with him, as usual.

A strange awareness tingled along her skin as Abby approached the copse of trees and bushes near the house. Her gaze was drawn to the man sitting on the bench under a crape myrtle tree. The deep green of his shirt blended with the leaves and fuchsia-colored blossoms of the tree, but his white slacks were a sharp contrast. She never would have used the term *beautiful* to describe a man, until she met Webb. No matter what he was wearing, no matter where he was, he commanded attention. He certainly had hers.

He was alone. After a brief hesitation, she walked over to him.

"Did Marilyn desert you?"

Sliding over to give her room to sit beside him, Webb asked casually, "Who's Marilyn?"

Abby declined to sit down, but remained standing

several feet away from him. "The blonde who was giving you a private tour."

"Some people arrived, so she's taking them around."

He didn't seem to be terribly disappointed. "Did you enjoy your tour with her?"

"She was very informative."

Abby had the impression she was missing something. Webb was looking at her with a curious expression. "I didn't know you were interested in the eighteenth century," she said.

"I was more interested in the present, and Marilyn was very helpful."

There was an underlying bitc in his tone that puzzled Abby. She didn't have time to solve puzzles. "If you are interested in the present, you've come to a strange place to find it. We sort of wallow in the past here."

Webb stood up and broke off a small sprig of crape myrtle from a low-hanging branch. Stopping only a breath away from her, he lightly brushed the colorful blossoms along her jawline.

His voice was like rich velvet as he asked, "Were eighteenth-century women all that different from women of today? Were they as complicated, as stubborn, and as intriguing as you are?"

Her fingers closed around his wrist, but he resisted her attempt to pull his hand away from her face. His other hand removed hers, and he laced his fingers through hers, bringing them down to his side. The soft petals trailed down her neck to the slight rise of her breasts exposed by the loose neckline of her shift.

Her eyes were caught by his, and she was unable to look away. "Don't," she begged raggedly.

"Don't what? Don't touch you? I have to. Don't

ask you questions? I have to, and I'll be asking a lot more later when I take you home."

Abby had the odd sensation she was sliding down a slippery hill, unable to get her footing, out of control of her own life. "Brenda is giving me a ride home."

He lifted her hand and placed the crape myrtle blossoms on her palm, then closed her fingers over them. He returned to the bench and sat back down. "I'll wait here for you. Brenda knows you'll be coming with me."

She was going to have to talk with him, too, about being so darned bossy, Abby thought as she returned to the house. Brenda and Marilyn were able to finish dipping the candles because there was a lull, leaving Abby free to do the necessary paper work of recording the admission fees and donations given to the restoration fund.

After the two other guides had left at five o'clock, Abby went outside to find Webb. He was talking with the caretaker, who was getting ready to mow the lawn now that the house was closed to visitors.

Webb saw her coming. "I'm shocked, Abby," he said. "A modern lawn mower on these hallowed grounds?"

Tom, the caretaker, took off his hat and wiped the perspiration off his brow. "I told him we were plumb out of goats, Miss Stout," he said with a wide grin.

"That we are, Tom." Meeting Webb's amused eyes, she explained, "The Historical Society has to make certain compromises. Not only do we resort to lawn mowers, but there is a smoke alarm in every room and a telephone in the office. We try to be factual but can't be fanatical."

Tom was chuckling as Webb took Abby's arm and led her away.

"You'll have to make another compromise, Abby," he said. "We're going by car instead of horse-drawn buggy."

As he pulled out of the parking lot, instead of turning left to go to Abby's house, he turned right.

"Where are you going?" she asked. "This is the wrong way."

"I have to stop at my office." He looked at her briefly. "Don't worry. I'll bring you home in plenty of time to get ready for work."

"I don't work tonight," she said, removing her cap. "The hotel has a string ensemble to play on Saturday nights."

This time Webb looked at her a little longer. They were making progress after all, he thought. Abby had actually volunteered the information instead of having it pried out of her. Maybe after his little experiment, she would open up that door in her mind marked "Private" and let him in.

"Do me a favor," he said softly.

For a smile like the one he sent her way, Abby would do anything. "What?"

"Take down your hair."

Her eyes locked with his for a long moment. When his attention returned to the road, she began removing the pins holding her heavy hair up in a knot on the top of her head. As she shook her head slightly to loosen the hair, her spirits soared, as if they, too, had been released from bondage. She felt lighter and more carefree than she had in a long time. She didn't even try to analyze it. She relaxed against the leather seat, not terribly concerned about their destination, leaving everything to Webb.

He had more than one destination. First Webb

pulled into a large parking lot where a number of navy blue trucks were parked, trucks with Hunter Construction painted on the doors.

"It's my turn to be tour guide," he said as he turned off the engine.

Abby was shown the heavy equipment parked behind a warehouse, the large inventory of building materials inside the warehouse, the reception area, his brother's office, and finally his own office.

Indicating one of the leather chairs in front of his desk, Webb invited her to sit down. "I have some papers to sign, then I'll take you home."

While his attention was on the papers, Abby looked around his office. There were several large-leafed plants in brass containers on the floor, filling the areas between a bookcase and a large, tilted drawing table against one wall. There was a shelf beneath the table that held several rolled-up blueprints, and the work area was illuminated by a fluorescent light.

The rustling of papers brought her gaze back to Webb. A frown of concentration creased his forehead as he studied one sheet. The room suited him, Abby concluded. It was the office of a meticulous man who liked order and professionalism.

Several brass picture frames were displayed on the low credenza behind him. In one, a man resembling Webb was holding a small child on his lap. Two older children, a boy and a girl, were sitting on the floor in front of him, along with a pretty, dark-haired woman. In another frame was a photo of the same man standing beside Webb, holding one end of a string of fish. The picture next to it was of an older couple. The man was an older, softer version of Webb.

Abby tore her gaze away from the family photos and studied Webb's features. He was a strong man with, she guessed, strong ties to his family. Part of his strength and confidence had no doubt been forged by the love of the people in those pictures.

Webb scrawled his name on the last letter he had to sign. He looked up to find Abby's serious green gaze on him. There was a strange, haunted sadness in the depths of her eyes, and he wondered why it was there.

"You ready to go?" he asked. "I'm finished here."

Nodding, Abby got to her feet.

Soon they were back in his car, and she tried to guess where he would stop next. The last place she expected was a Chinese restaurant.

He parked near the pagoda-shaped door. "I'll be back in a minute. There's something in the glove compartment to keep you company while I'm gone."

She stared after him as he strode through the red door of the restaurant. Then, curious, she pushed the button on the glove compartment and removed the crumpled tissue-paper bundle from inside. She carefully unwrapped the paper, uncovering a sleeping teddy bear wearing blue-and-white-striped pajamas. He was lying on his tummy, with his rear end up in the air, his hind legs tucked underneath. A tag tied to one foot read "Clarence."

Clarence was snoozing peacefully on her lap when Webb returned with a bulging shopping bag that had the logo of the restaurant emblazoned on it. Delicious odors emanated from it.

He set the bag on the back seat, then glanced down at her lap as he slid behind the wheel. "I see you've met Clarence."

She smiled teasingly. "There's something about him that reminds me of you."

"Really?" Webb grimaced. "I'm going to regret this,

but what could I possibly have in common with Clarence? I'm not fuzzy and I don't wear pajamas."

That last fascinating bit of information almost made Abby forget the point she was trying to make. "I don't mean there's a physical resemblance, although Clarence does have long, sexy lashes like yours." She ignored the choking sound that turned into a cough. "It's more an attitude."

"An attitude? How can I have the same attitude as a stuffed bear, who, I might point out, is sleeping, while I am wide awake?"

Abby held up Clarence. "Look at him. He's doing what he wants to do. Sleeping. Even if we would rather he was awake, he sleeps."

Webb looked at her as if she had popped her last cork. "I think your funny little cap was on too tight, Abigail. You aren't making much sense."

"Yes, I am. You just don't want to see it. Let me put it another way. Look at him from where you're sitting. You are in the driver's seat and I'm along for the ride. Like Clarence, you are doing as you damn please."

"Don't swear, Abigail," Webb scolded as he started the engine. "It's not ladylike."

"Horse feathers."

"That's better," he said complacently as he pulled away from the restaurant.

Glaring at him with the fiercest expression she could muster didn't do a lot of good, since he kept his attention on the road. She crossed her arms and refused to say another word. She had said it herself; she was along for the ride.

"Now, Abby, don't pout. We'll have a nice long chat over the Moo Goo Gai Pan. You can point out the error of my ways to your heart's content. Be patient until then."

Patience had never been one of her virtues, but she found enough to get by on until they arrived at her house. Her car was parked in the driveway. At least it resembled her car, except for four shiny new tires and a polished sheen covering the fading paint.

"The keys are over the visor," was the only comment Webb made when he saw her staring at the car on their way to her front door.

She was about to demand they have a chat as soon as she unlocked her door—she could ask him how much she owed him for the car repairs—but he had a different suggestion.

"You go change into something from the twentieth century and I'll get this stuff spread out."

Amazing, she thought as she nodded. He kept giving her orders and she kept obeying them. This had to stop. She was going to have to put her foot down . . . or something.

In her bedroom, she reached for a pair of jeans and an oversized cotton sweater, stubbornly choosing to wear her usual comfortable clothes instead of dressing up just because Webb was there. It was just as well she was unaware of how the jean hugged her hips and how provocative the large sweater would be to a man interested in what lay underneath.

A staggering variety of Oriental dishes in white cardboard containers was spread out on the table when Abby entered the kitchen. Webb was rummaging through a drawer.

"What are you looking for?" she asked.

"I'm not that handy with chopsticks. I'm looking for forks."

She opened another drawer and took out two forks and a handful of serving spoons. Webb had already found glasses and had poured white wine into two of them. He took the spoons from her and began to dish the food onto their plates.

He paused when he realized she hadn't moved, and his hands went to his hips again as he looked at her. "Are you going to eat standing up?"

"I was waiting to be told to sit down," she said with mock sweetness.

Smiling broadly, he pulled out a chair for her and leaned over to kiss her lightly on the nose. "You're so cute when you get uppity. Put your dragon on hold for a while. I'm hungry."

He was impossible! But she was very hungry, too, so she sat down and began to eat. Some of the dishes were new to her, but she tried every one of them, unaware of the satisfied gleam in Webb's eyes.

Finally she put down her fork and leaned back in her chair. "I haven't the faintest idea what I ate, but it was delicious."

A fortune cookie was placed on her empty plate. "No Chinese meal is complete until you read your fortune."

She broke open the cookie and took out the thin strip of paper tucked inside. She read silently. "Be thrifty to prepare today for the wants of tomorrow." Well, that wasn't too far off the mark. She had been preparing for something she had wanted for a long time. What would Webb think if he knew why she had been going without meals and working herself into the ground? She wasn't ready to find out. Not yet. Not until she knew what lay behind his lord-and-master routine.

At his request, she read the fortune aloud to him. He didn't think much of it. "They don't make fortunes like they used to," he said disgustedly. "Whatever happened to 'You will meet a tall, dark, handsome man who will sweep you off your feet'?"

She already had and he already had. Technically, he had stepped on her foot, but his kisses had definitely swept her away. "Open yours," she said. "Maybe your fortune will be better. Maybe something about a bosomy blonde."

The fortune cookie broke open with a snap. "Why does everyone think I go for blondes?"

"Don't you prefer blondes?" He had been with one that night at the hotel.

He gazed at her vibrant-colored hair. "Not exclusively." He drew out the sliver of paper from one half of the cookie and read aloud, "The rider likes best the horse that needs breaking in."

"That doesn't sound like Confucius to me."

"Whoever wrote it, I agree with the thought."

"You like a challenge?"

"Apparently," he said dryly. "I'm hanging out with you, aren't I?"

She choked on a laugh. "I'm not a challenge. Just an ordinary person who is going to clean up this mess." She pushed her chair back and started shoving the empty containers back into the shopping bag.

Webb set their plates in the sink. "An ordinary person who keeps so busy, she doesn't have time for little things like eating and sleeping. The challenge comes in trying to figure out why you want to be Wonder Woman."

Brushing past him, she turned on the water and squirted a generous amount of dishwashing liquid into the sink. "I'm not trying to be Wonder Woman. I'm just trying to get by."

"Between taking classes in history, writing your thesis for your master's degree, being assistant director of Bristol House, and playing piano five nights a week, you 'get by' with more than a full schedule."

With her hands in the sudsy water, she paused and looked over her shoulder at him. "I'm not the only one who's been busy."

He came to stand beside her, leaning his slim hip against the counter. "Marilyn was very helpful once she got going on the subject of the clever, hardworking Abigail Stout. She's quite a fan."

"She was supposed to talk about Bristol House, not me."

He captured a lock of her hair, curling the end around his finger. "I was more interested in you than in Bristol House." His gaze left her hair to meet her wary green eyes. "Learning about you is not an easy task. I have to take advantage of every opportunity I can."

When she remained silent, he continued, "What else do you do, Abby? Fly jets on the weekends?"

She lifted a soapy hand to remove his hand from her hair. "You don't need to get nasty."

He grabbed her hand and held on to it, soap and all. "You haven't seen nasty yet." With a short jerk, he spun her around, ignoring the dampness on his chest as she tried to push him away with her other hand.

"You would have seen nasty after I heard about your other activities from Marilyn. From Marilyn, not you. Why, Abby? Why do I have to discover important things about you by accident or from someone else? I get crumbs, when I want, need, the whole loaf. Talk to me, for Pete's sake."

His degree of anger shocked Abby. Along with the anger, he appeared hurt because she hadn't confided in him. He also acted as if he had a right to know everything about her.

"Do you expect to hear the life story of every woman you know?" she asked defensively.

"No," he said quietly, the anger draining away. "Only yours. I took you to my office today so you could see an important aspect of my life. I was hoping that if I shared part of my life, you would feel freer about sharing some of yours with me."

His expression was intense and determined. She couldn't look away. "I don't understand why knowing everything about me is so important to you."

"Maybe this will help." He lowered his head and kissed her softly, sensually. The intimate warmth of her mouth drew him into her to taste and savor her, absorbing her moan of pleasure.

Pulling away slowly, he placed his hands on her hips to keep her close but their bodies apart. "I can read your responses when I touch you, but I can't read your mind."

His kiss had disintegrated her usual reticence. "I'm not used to talking about myself."

"With anyone or with men?"

"With anyone." She gave him a half-smile. "There haven't been a lot of men."

"With your schedule, I'm not surprised. In case you haven't noticed, I'm not intimidated by your schedule."

"I noticed."

"If we're to have any type of relationship, you at least have to let me in on the basics of your life. I don't necessarily have to know how often you brush your teeth, but I would like some idea of how you live."

"Exactly what kind of relationship are we supposed to be having?"

He leaned down and kissed her briefly. "The best kind there is." He released her and picked up a dish towel. "The kind of relationship where you wash and I dry."

Throaty laughter bubbled up from inside her, and her eyes were brilliant with amusement. "That makes as much sense as anything."

It was the first time he had ever heard her laugh, really laugh. It was a sound he wanted to hear often.

He had dried the two glasses and was wiping off a plate when she said, "You're no amateur with that dish towel."

"I've had a lot of practice. There's one hitch to cadging meals at my brother's. I get dish towel duty. My brother is one of those cooks who can't put a meal together unless he's emptied the cupboards of every dish and bowl. They have a dishwasher, but Brad always tells me it doesn't work."

"Your brother does the cooking?"

"He wants his three children to survive their childhood. Ellen is a lousy cook. Plus Brad likes to cook."

Abby handed him the last plate. "Do you like to cook too?"

"I manage to get by on the basics. My one outstanding contribution to the culinary arts is the meanest chili this side of the Texas state line. I don't fix it often, because I've grown rather fond of my stomach lining."

She wrung out the dishrag as he carried two glasses, and the wine bottle into the living room. She trailed after him and sat down beside him on the couch, one leg tucked under her. He poured the wine and handed her a glass.

Whether it was the meal, the wine, or the company, Abby was content to sit and do nothing for a change. Her gaze rested on his hand holding a glass of wine. She remembered how her skin had felt when that hand stroked it, and wanted to feel like that again. Her body might be relaxing, but her imagination was working overtime.

"What's your specialty, Abby?"

Startled by the sudden question when her mind had been on other things, she looked at him in confusion. "Excuse me?"

"Cooking. We were talking about cooking." Noticing the slight tinge of embarrassed color in her cheeks, he added, "At least, I was talking about cooking. Now I'm curious as to what you were thinking about."

Grabbing for the safer topic, she said, "Thanks to some of the foster homes I've lived in, I can cook most Italian dishes, some Mexican food, and know forty ways to fix hamburger. Mrs. Romano insisted we girls all learn to measure the spices in the palms of our hands, and I constantly smelled like a clove of garlic. Mrs. Sanchez made me learn to make tortillas from scratch. The first couple of time that I tried to flatten them with my hands the way she did, they turned out to be inedible Frisbees."

"And the forty ways to cook hamburger?"

"That was Mrs. Randall. Along with three foster children, she had five children of her own. Hamburger was the cheapest meat she could get that we would eat, so we had it a variety of ways. When I left there, I stayed away from hamburger for six months."

"How many foster homes were you in?"

"Too many." She swirled the wine around in his glass, watching the pale liquid sparkle in the light. "I was not what you might call an adorable child. I believe the correct word is incorrigible. I rebelled against living with people who were being paid to put up with me."

It was easy for Webb to imagine a much younger Abby battling against a charitable existence, her proud chin tilted upward. "Your dragon appeared early," he said.

There was no evidence of pity or sympathy in his

face or voice. If there had been any sign of either, she wouldn't have been able to go on. As it was, she found it easier to talk about her past than she had thought it would be. "I suppose I've had my independence from the day I was abandoned. When I realized I wouldn't be adopted, I decided I had to work to get whatever I wanted. So, I work."

"You certainly do." He set his glass down and shifted slightly, turning toward her with his arm across the back of the couch. "What I don't understand is why you weren't snapped up by some couple who were in the market for a spirited little redhead."

Abby found herself smiling, making light of a once-sensitive subject. She was surprised at how easy it was to say aloud. "A little girl with a pip of an overbite and a giant chip on her skinny shoulder. Thanks to an expensive orthodontist and a couple of years of wearing braces, I no longer have the overbite." She paused. "I'm still working on the chip."

His strong hand moved to her shoulder, smoothing over the slender bones. "I don't feel anything but you."

"Trust me. It's there." Suddenly she gazed at him in near shock, realizing how much she had told him. "Why am I telling you all this?"

He slid his hand around her throat, his thumb gently stroking the sensitive spot below her ear. "Because you know I want to hear it."

She started to draw back from him, but he wouldn't allow that. "I used to crave caramels and chewing gum," he said, "even though I had never particularly liked either one before I became a metal mouth."

Her eyes widened in astonishment, and she looked at his mouth. When he bared his straight white teeth at her, she barely suppressed a laugh. "*You* wore braces?"

He nodded. "It was either wear braces or get used to my brother calling me Bugs for the rest of my life. He, the rat, had perfect teeth. Fortunately there were a lot of other fourteen- and fifteen-year-old kids with flashy smiles. I remember trying to kiss Marcia Theobald at a school dance and nearly getting my braces caught on hers."

Abby smiled easily, responding to his admission. "I was twenty-two. I adopted a peculiar grimace in place of a natural smile for the first six months. Eventually I reverted to a normal smile when I realized I was scaring the customers at the restaurant where I was playing piano. Since my salary and tips were paying for those blasted braces, I couldn't afford to alienate the clientele. On campus, there were more unusual sights than my braces, and I gradually got over being self-conscious about them."

Webb stared at her, somewhat in awe. His father had simply written out a check to pay for his orthodontic work, and had paid for college tuition for both his sons. How had Abby managed to accomplish so much by sheer grit and determination? He had his parents to thank for providing him with security and an education. Abby had no one but herself.

"Do you have any idea how exceptional you are, Abby?"

"I'm not"—her breath caught as his hand glided up over her neck and jaw until his thumb came to rest on her bottom lip—"exceptional," she finished. Her tongue darted out to moisten her suddenly dry lips, accidentally stroking the rough skin of his thumb.

A smoky haze came into his eyes as the mere

touch of her tongue sent liquid fire through his body. His hands cupped her face, holding her still. "You are exceptional, courageous, and the most beautiful woman I've ever known."

"You don't have to say things like that to me, Webb," she murmured seriously. "I know who I am and what I am."

His lips lightly brushed hers. "You haven't the faintest idea who and what you are if you think I'm wrong." He pulled back to see her clearly. "The ugly duckling has turned into a swan, but you've been too tired and overworked to see it. You also can't see I'm interested in you, your life, your work, your thoughts, your feelings, everything about you."

His hands slid down over her shoulders to her breasts, his dark gaze remaining on her face. "No. Don't pull away from me, Abby. I'm only showing you how beautiful you feel to me."

Whatever he was looking for in her eyes, he apparently found it. He covered her mouth with his, pleased when her lips parted. He slipped his fingers beneath her sweater as he deepened the kiss.

He eased her down onto the plump cushions, savoring the thrust of her breasts against his chest. His name was a breathless sigh from her lips as, with his mouth, he sampled the delicate skin of her neck. The explosive current of desire invaded his senses, making his head swim.

Abby's hands found his hard, broad chest and shoulders, then roamed across his powerful back. They clenched involuntarily as his own hands slid under her hips. She was rocked by an incredibly painful pleasure as he brought her body more intimately into the cradle of his hips.

Then his hand slowly covered one of her breasts. She gasped raggedly. He caught her breath in his mouth as he took her lips boldly, fiercely, while his fingers caressed her soft flesh. The intoxicating feel of her under him was dissolving the little control he had left.

The realization hit him hard. What in hell was he doing? Dammit, he was out of his mind. To take her now would be wrong. Right for him, but wrong for her.

Abruptly, he pulled her arms from around his neck and pushed his long body off her. "I'm sorry, Abby," he said hoarsely. "I didn't mean to go so far with you."

Sitting on the edge of the couch, he gently tugged her sweater down to her waist, a strange look in his eyes as he covered her bare flesh.

Abby didn't move. She couldn't. She stared at his tight mouth, saw the rigid way he held himself, and misunderstood his withdrawal. Had she done something wrong? she wondered. Why was he was rejecting her?

Feeling slightly sick from the sudden shift from heaven to hell, she moved quickly. She drew her knees up to her chest and huddled against the corner of the couch. She lifted her chin and stared at him steadily. Her pride wouldn't allow her to let him see her misery and confusion. "One nice thing about messing around with orphans," she said, "is that there's no father with a shotgun in the background."

His jaw clenched. "I wasn't messing around with you," he snapped. "You make it sound like a cheap seduction scene."

Discussing it was like rubbing salt in an open wound. She wanted to end it and be alone to heal the tear he had made deep inside her. "Whatever you want to call it, it's over. Nothing happened, so let's drop it."

Webb wished he could read her mind. He had an uneasy feeling about the way she was taking this.

He reached out to her, but she scrambled off the couch. "I'd stay away from Chinese food if I were you. It seems to have an amorous effect on you."

She was standing several feet away, her arms folded defensively in front of her. The proud tilt of her chin told him to back off, but he didn't want to leave things the way they were. He had handled the situation badly. He knew that. Now wasn't the time to make it up to her. Not while his body was aching for her. He might make things worse the minute he touched her again.

"All right, Abby," he said wearily. "I'll go. Walk me to the door."

Abby blinked. It wasn't what she had expected.

At the door, he hesitated. Looking down at her, he said, "It wasn't the Chinese food, Abby. It was you."

His mouth grazed hers. "I hope you sleep better than I will," he murmured. "Lock the door."

One moment he was there, and the next he was gone. Abby automatically locked the door, her mind as confused and bewildered as her deprived body. Knowing it would be impossible to sleep right away, she dragged out her research books to find a reference she needed for her thesis. After a short time, she closed the book she had been leafing through.

It was no use. All she could think about was Webb Hunter. Damn him. She had carefully planned each hour, each day, each dollar spent or saved. There had been no contingency plan for an impossible man who made her forget everything but him.

The main problem was, she had no idea why he kept coming back to see her, kissing her, confusing her when she needed to think straight. She had no idea what he was thinking or feeling about her, and it was impossible even to try to guess.

The choices came down to continuing as she had before Webb had stomped into her life, or accepting whatever he wanted to give. It no longer made sense that he was seeing her because of some quixotic feeling of guilt or pity. Was she a challenge to him, the horse that needed breaking in?

It was a long time before she managed to fall asleep that night.

Six

Clarence and the other teddy bears on the dresser were the first thing Abby saw when she opened her eyes. Grimacing at the reminder of Webb, she rolled over onto her stomach and punched the pillow. Then she pulled the covers over her head to shut out the early-morning light coming through the window.

After a few minutes, she sighed with impatience and flung back the covers. She looked at the clock on the bedside table. Five-thirty.

She groaned. The one morning she could sleep in, and she wasn't able to. It wasn't fair. She wanted to sleep. She needed sleep. The few extra hours of much-needed sleep on Sunday mornings kept her going through the rest of the week.

She might as well get up and do something useful, now that she was awake. After untangling her feet from the bedclothes, she stood beside the bed and looked down at the jumbled sheets and blanket, proof of her restless night. Losing sleep hadn't solved a thing. Going over every word spoken between herself and Webb hadn't made the end of the evening any clearer. She would have been better off sleeping. Unfortunately she hadn't been able to shut off her thoughts.

Instead of wasting any more time, she decided to work on her thesis. The eighteenth century was easier to understand than the present. And she had to concentrate on her goal. The only way she was going to achieve it was by finishing her thesis and getting her degree. It was the last step down the long road toward having someone of her own, a baby to whom she could give all the love she had.

She was still in her nightshirt at seven o'clock, when the doorbell rang. She was tempted to ignore it. Maudie always came to the back door, and she wasn't expecting anyone else, especially at that hour of the morning.

Whoever it was gave up on the doorbell and started knocking instead.

Throwing down her pen, Abby shoved the chair back from the kitchen table. She would get rid of the early bird and spend the entire day on her history paper.

She looked through the peephole to see who was there, but all she saw was part of an old hat with all sorts of fishing lures and hooks stuck into the band. What in the world? She grabbed her trench coat out of the hall closet and slipped it on to cover her scanty nightshirt.

Cautiously she opened the door. A huge teddy bear blocked the doorway. He was wearing a droopy fishing hat and holding a fishing rod in one paw. A placard was hanging around his neck, which read: "Wanna go fishin?"

A masculine hand was holding on to one paw to keep the bear upright. Abby's gaze followed past the hand, up an arm covered in blue cotton, across a tan, fisherman's vest, up to amused gray eyes.

Webb studied her trench coat and bare feet. "Expecting rain?"

Abby closed her mouth, which had gaped open as soon as she saw the bear. Then she opened it again to speak. "I had to put something on to answer the door. What are you and"—she pointed at the bear—"it doing here?"

Webb had a peculiar expression on his face. "What do you have on under the coat?"

Giving him a quelling glance, she snapped, "Enough."

Reprimanding himself for thinking about the body underneath that coat when he should be concentrating on persuading her to spend the day with him, Webb finally got around to answering her question. "Beauregard and I are going fishing. We thought you might like to come along."

Her lips trembled as she tried not to smile. "Beauregard?"

"Beau for short."

It was impossible to hold it in any longer. Her laughter floated in the air, giving pleasure to the man in front of her. "You are crazy. A certifiable loony. You and . . . ah, Beau had better come in before the neighbors call the happy wagon to come and cart you away."

Beau was lifted off the porch and repositioned against a chair in the living room. "Maudie already knows about Beau," Webb said. "She was with me when I bought him."

Abby had to sit down. "Maudie went with you to buy a teddy bear? We're talking about the lady next door?"

Webb perched on the arm of the couch, facing the

chair she had collapsed into, and casually crossed one jean-clad leg over the other at the ankle. "We bought Beau after we had lunch." He grinned at Abby's astounded expression. "Maudie had a great time picking out a pudgy stuffed goose to take home to Ira. Apparently Ira had a pet goose as a child and Maudie thought he would like a reminder of it."

The roller-coaster ride had started up again, and Abby felt both exhilarated and petrified by Webb. She held her hand up. "Wait a minute. Back up. One thing at a time." Taking a deep, steadying breath, she asked, "You took Maudie to lunch?"

"Yesterday. Before I came out to Bristol House."

"Why would you take Maudie to lunch?"

"To pump her for information about you. She neglected to tell me you didn't have to work on Saturday nights. I hope she wasn't wrong about today. Beau and I want to take you fishing."

Abby straightened the lapels of her coat, feeling incredibly foolish and uncomfortably warm in the coat. Still, fiddling with the lapels gave her something to do while she was deep in thought. Finally she said, "After last night . . ."

He was suddenly in front of her chair, pulling her upright. "I was unbelievably clumsy last night, Abby. It wasn't until I got home that it dawned on me just how you had misinterpreted my pulling away from you." He tilted her chin up. "I didn't stop because I didn't want you. I stopped because I *did* want you."

"Then why did you stop?" she asked softly.

"Abby," he said gruffly, "what are you trying to tell me?"

"That I'm a big girl now. I knew what would happen if you continued to kiss me."

"Are you saying you wanted me too?"

She had gone this far. She might as well continue. "I thought that was obvious."

"Miss Abby," he drawled. "I have discovered there is nothing obvious about you. It's strictly trial and error."

"So where do we go from here?"

His hands slid down to the lapels of her coat. "We go fishing. You'll have to ditch the raincoat, though. The weather forecast calls for sunny skies, not a drop of rain."

"You're serious!"

"About fishing? Deadly serious."

Torn between what she should do and what she wanted to do, she said hesitantly, "I was working on my thesis."

"My reliable source of information from next door has told me you rarely, if ever, take any time for some rest and relaxation. You're overdue. All work and no play will make Abby a dreary girl."

"Dull."

"What?"

"Make Abby a dull girl."

"Never dull. You are a lot of things, Abby, but not dull." He gave her a gentle push in the direction of her bedroom. "Go change and dig up a bathing suit."

She balked. "I've never been fishing in my life."

He gave her a horrified look. "You're kidding!" When she shook her head, he said firmly, "We'll have to fill that gap in your education. Fortunately you will have a superior instructor to show you how. Now, get a move on."

She moved. As she dressed in khaki shorts and a red knit top, she felt a glow of anticipation. It wasn't the prospect of fishing that caused it, but the thought of spending an entire day with Webb. Life had taught her to grab the brass ring whenever she had the opportunity, in case it didn't come around again.

This one she was going to grab. She would have the memories of today to bring out when Webb had moved on . . . as he inevitably would.

Beau had to be left behind. The cab of Webb's pickup truck wasn't big enough to comfortably accommodate them and a plump bear. As they drove toward the mountains, Webb explained that he had brought the truck because the terrain required a four-wheel-drive vehicle.

Abby saw what he meant when he turned onto a rough strip of road, barely wide enough for the truck. Branches hit the windows and scraped the sides as they bounced along. After several curves, Webb stopped the truck beside a log cabin nestled among towering pine trees.

Abby stared through the windshield at the shimmering lake about fifty feet from the cabin. A wooden raft was floating some distance out, on the dark blue surface. There was no sign of other cabins, and the only dock projecting from the shoreline was the one in front of Webb's cabin. It was as though the rest of the world had been left behind when they had turned off the paved road.

She wasn't aware that Webb had gotten out of the truck until he opened her door. She reluctantly looked away from the lake to meet Webb's amused gaze.

"It's beautiful," she exclaimed, her voice full of awe.

"I'm glad you like it. I was hoping you would."

"It was worth going over that washboard of a road to get here, even though I may never sit down again. Why don't you bring one of those grader things I saw behind your warehouse and smooth out this road?"

He began to unload some boxes and gear out of the back of the truck. "If I brought a road grader up here to clear a decent road, people driving by might be curious where the road went. This way I have the privacy I want without any snoopy people butting in." He handed her several fishing poles. "Here. You carry these and I'll bring the rest. Look out for the hook."

His warning came too late. Abby let out a yelp, and he dropped the tackle box to help her.

He deftly removed the hook from the soft part of her palm, giving her the impression he had done this sort of thing before. When he was through he calmly turned back to retrieve the tackle box.

"Gee, this fishing *is* fun," she said brightly, looking warily at the first-aid box he was including with the other equipment. Not wanting to dwell on the possible reasons a first-aid kit would be necessary when fishing, she studied some of the other things he had brought.

"What's in the Styrofoam containers with the holes punched in the tops?" she asked.

"Worms."

Luckily Webb had started toward the door of the cabin and didn't see the face Abby made. Giving the containers a wide berth, she followed him. He set the equipment down inside the cabin and met her at the door. Taking the fishing poles from her, he leaned them against the outside wall by the door.

"I'll give you a quick tour of the cabin before we get the boat out," he said.

Stepping inside, Abby immediately forgot about hooks, worms, and going out in a boat. The inside walls were like the outside, logs with strips of white caulking between them. A braided rug covered a large part of the floor of the main room, between a wooden couch and two chairs with plaid cushions. A stone fireplace took up the better part of one wall, with a section made into a small cave for storing firewood. In the back was a tiny kitchen. A hand pump was attached to the sink for water, and an old wood stove stood by the back entrance.

Leading her back into the living room, Webb pointed toward a rope dangling down from an open loft area. "The rope pulls down a folding ladder for access to the bedroom, but I haven't finished that room yet. I use a sleeping bag in front of the fire for now."

She turned to look at him instead of the loft. "You built this cabin?"

"Am building this cabin," he corrected her. "It sort of keeps growing. Each time I think I'm done, I get another idea." He smiled at her, a speculative gleam in his eyes. "Take the bedroom, for example. Suddenly I have this itch to get it completed."

She hadn't missed the sensual curve of his smile. "Feeling sleepy?" she asked teasingly.

"Not . . . exactly." He looked at her long and hard, the amusement gone from his expression. Every time he looked at her, he thought, he wanted her. The need to make her his got stronger whenever he was with her. He forced his desire aside and smiled. "Let's go fishing."

It didn't take Webb long to uncover the aluminum fishing boat. Once Abby and the fishing equipment had been deposited in it, he shoved it into the water. He motored out to some distance away from shore, then shut off the engine and dropped anchor. He showed Abby how to bait her hook, and once she got over the squeamies from touching the worm, she began to enjoy fishing. In fact, as the morning wore on she was catching more fish than the superior instructor. Webb took it very well, eventually leaning back against the motor to watch her animated face as she reeled in fish after fish.

When the sun was high, he suggested they return to shore. There were more than enough fish for their lunch. The mention of lunch made Abby realize how hungry she was. The combination of fresh air, sunshine, and exercise had all worked together to whip up a ravenous appetite.

Once back on shore, Webb led her to a cleared area near the cabin. Stones had been arranged in a circle around a shallow pit, and he laid a fire there. After cleaning the fish, he placed a wire grate across the stones, then set on top of that a frying pan full of the fish. There wasn't much for Abby to do once she had spread out a blanket and set out the plates, silverware, a container of store-bought potato salad, and bags of potato chips Webb had brought.

She sat back and watched him, noticing the taut muscles in his thighs as he knelt near the fire. He had removed the vest and rolled up the sleeves of his work shirt. The outdoors suited him, she thought. The wind ruffled his hair as it rustled through the pine trees around them. He looked very much at home here, at peace with himself and his surroundings.

The easy, natural way he had made the fire and set to work cooking their lunch made it apparent he had done this type of thing many times before.

"You lied to me," she said out of the blue.

His head jerked up, and he looked surprised. "I lied to you? When?"

"When you said the only thing you can cook is chili. You aren't doing too badly with that fish."

He went back to flipping the sizzling fish. "I told you I can manage the basics. You can't get more basic than cooking over an open fire. I should make you cook them, since you caught most of them. Are you sure you've never been fishing before?"

"Positive." She nibbled on a potato chip. "I have a confession to make." He looked up at her again. "I didn't think I was going to like fishing, especially when you brought out the wiggly worms."

"And now?"

"I enjoyed it. It's not as difficult as I expected it to be."

A slightly pained expression crossed his face briefly. "You do seem to have a knack for catching fish," he said dryly.

"Beginner's luck. I also had a good teacher."

He rewarded her with a warm smile. "My ego thanks you."

When they were done he piled the fried fish on a blue-and-white-splattered tin pie plate and brought them over to the blanket. He spooned several of the golden-brown fish onto a tin plate and handed the plate to her, then served himself.

"I had hoped," he said as he sat Indian-style on the blanket, "to impress you with my prowess as a fisherman, but I ended up being the one impressed. It looks like I had better come up with some other clever plan."

"Why do you think you have to impress me?"

"Because I've made one mistake after the other with you. I don't understand it. I'm usually the guy with all the answers, a smooth-tongued son-of-a-gun. With you, I stomp all over your feet, boss you around, and demand you do this and that. A supermacho jerk. I thought that by bringing you here, I might impress you with my back-to-nature qualities."

"You've succeeded." More than he could have planned. The glimpse of vulnerability in his desire to show her a different side of himself was touching. "For one man to build all of this with his own hands is very impressive. To want to build a cabin in a place of such beauty and to want to keep it all to himself is equally impressive."

"I don't necessarily want to keep it all to myself. I'm just selective about who I invite here."

"So I'm an exception?"

He laughed. "That you are. In more ways than one. The only other person I've had up here is my brother. He came one weekend to help me put up the rafters."

Abby was pleased she was the only woman he had brought to his hideaway. "I would think your brother would want to bring his family up here."

"Ellen's idea of camping out is taking a room at the Ramada Inn. Come to think of it, that's Brad's idea of roughing it too." Tossing his empty plate onto the blanket, he said, "You catch some tasty fish, Miss Abby."

"You fry up some tasty fish, Mr. Webb."

He abruptly changed course. "How do you feel about a hammock?"

"A hammock," she repeated vaguely. Then, a little heatedly, she said, "Do you realize how often you jump from one subject to another? It's like trying to talk to a hyper frog."

He laughed. "Sorry. I have always preferred short-cuts to taking the long way around." He uncoiled his long legs and got to his feet. He started walking toward the truck, saying over his shoulder, "You'll get used to it."

Maybe, she thought. If—No, she wasn't going to think of any *if*'s today. She gathered up the remains of their picnic, setting the plates and silverware to one side. By the time she had the leftovers in a box and had folded the blanket, Webb was coming back with his arms full of a mass of woven rope.

While he returned to the cabin for a hammer and

some nails, she washed the dishes in the lake. She could have done them in the kitchen, but it was too lovely out in the fresh air and sunshine to bother going indoors.

On her way back, she heard several colorful words usually reserved for the locker room. She came up over the rise and saw Webb standing between two sturdy trees, tugging and swearing at the tangled strands of rope.

"Lose the instructions?" she asked mildly.

"Very funny. Grab that section by my left foot. I think it goes through this part I'm holding."

Kneeling, Abby did as she was instructed. She was having a difficult time keeping a straight face.

"Now hold on to that one and I'll try this one under those two."

The ends of the hammock went under, over, through, between, and around. The only thing that was accomplished was to get Abby as snarled as Webb. Somehow, with all the contortions, she ended up sitting on his lap, wrapped tightly against his chest.

She couldn't hold her amusement in any longer. She started giggling, then laughed merrily at their predicament. After a moment Webb joined her. They laughed so hard, they toppled over, with Webb sprawled on the ground and Abby on top of him. His arms were tangled in the ropes around her waist and back, binding them together.

Their laughter slowly died as their eyes met and held. The intimacy of their position was having an unmistakable affect on Webb. Abby wasn't immune to the tension throbbing between them either. Mesmerized by the smoldering flame in his eyes, she slowly lowered her head to capture his mouth with hers. It was the first time she had taken the initiative and it stunned both of them. Her kiss was tentative at first, until his lips stirred under hers, encouraging her, daring her to explore his mouth.

Her bare legs grazed against the coarse material of his jeans as she shifted restlessly. The touch of the sun on her back was cool, compared to the scalding heat wherever her body touched his. When she heard a low moan of satisfaction from Webb, she felt an odd triumph. It was incredible to think she could draw a response from him.

Somehow a trace of common sense made its way forward, and she was shocked at her aggressiveness. She tore her mouth from his and buried her face against his neck.

His voice was soft against her hair. "As much as I'm enjoying this, we have to get out of these ropes." He smiled. "Unless you want to kiss me again."

She lifted her head but didn't meet his eyes. "We haven't been terribly successful so far," she said, referring to their problem and not the kiss.

"It depends on what you call success." He paused before murmuring her name in an odd tone. The sudden change from humor to hesitancy caused her to look at him, puzzled.

"What is it?" she asked.

"Promise you won't get mad?"

"About what?"

"I'm not going to tell you unless you promise you won't let fire with that temper of yours."

"All right. I promise."

Smiling up at her, he moved his arms in several directions and the ropes all fell away.

Abby rolled off him and bolted to her feet. "You—We could have gotten free at any time! What do you think I am, a calf at a rodeo?"

"Now, Abby, you promised you wouldn't get mad," he said calmly as he sat up.

"So sue me. That was a sneaky thing to do. I can't believe you got us all tangled up on purpose."

He stood up, bringing one end of the rope with him. "It didn't start out that way. By the time I had it almost untangled, you were on my lap. Then I was in no hurry to unwrap the ties that bound us."

Her anger ebbed away as she admitted to herself that she really had no complaints. She had enjoyed the experience too. "Your macho side is showing again."

He nodded in agreement as he tied the rope around the tree nearby. "It comes in handy once in a while." He picked up the other end of the rope and tied it securely to the other tree. The hammock swung gently, suspended between the trees, a few feet off the ground. Standing back, he gestured for her to try it out.

She shook her head. "Oh, no, you don't. It's your brilliant idea and your hammock."

"Ladies first."

Her eyes narrowed suspiciously. "If it's going to collapse, I'd rather you were in it. Besides, after that last stunt, I don't trust you."

"I wasn't the one who took advantage of the situation," he replied mildly. "Not that I'm complaining." Chuckling at the tint of color on her cheeks, he took her arm and pulled her toward the hammock. "We'll try it out together."

Before she could protest, she was hoisted off her feet by strong hands at her waist and plunked down in the middle of the hammock. Her weight caused it to sag, and she held on for dear life.

He flung one leg over the width of the hammock, straddling it before he leaned back, bringing her with him as he cautiously lifted one leg, then the other, off the ground. "So far so good."

Abby had a death grip on his shirt as they swayed back and forth, the ropes creaking in protest.

"Do seasick pills come with this thing?" she asked.

He chuckled, putting his arm around her. "It will calm down in a minute. Lie still."

He was lying on his back and she was on her side next to him, one arm flung across his waist. "I think I'd rather go fishing."

"You already caught all the fish."

The rope cradle was settling into a gentle rocking motion, more soothing than threatening, but Abby still was not sure they wouldn't be tossed out on their rear ends. "How about going swimming?"

"We just ate. You aren't supposed to go swimming right after you eat."

"You're no fun." She felt his body relax and heard his sigh of contentment. "Are you going to sleep?"

"Probably, unless you want to kiss me again. That would wake me up."

"It is peaceful here," she murmured.

The swaying motion of the hammock, the gentle breeze stirring the pine needles overhead, and the lapping of the small waves on the shore were making her incredibly drowsy. Her head rested comfortably on Webb's shoulder as he adjusted his hold on her.

She drifted off to sleep, her arm draped over his chest.

Webb didn't sleep. Even if he had gotten as little sleep as Abby had the past week, he doubted he would be able to sleep with her in his arms. He wanted to make love to her for hours, to satisfy this overwhelming need for her.

He wasn't sure how much longer he was going to be able to deny this physical craving that ate at him. A man only had so much control, especially when a woman responded to him as Abby did.

An hour later, Abby became aware of a series of delicious butterflylike kisses around her mouth. With her eyes still closed, she searched and finally found Webb's mouth with her own. Her senses came awake as his tongue surged into the velvety softness of her mouth. His masculine scent blended with the pine-scented air. What a wonderful way to wake up, she thought. Or maybe she was only dreaming. No, this wasn't a dream after all. The warm hand sliding across her rib cage was very real.

Webb felt a fierce tug of desire, an intoxicating pleasure radiating through him. He had planned to wake Abby softly with a kiss, but her immediate response demanded more from him. Forgetting for a moment where they were, he shifted his weight onto his side. The hammock swayed precariously.

He lifted his head and looked down into her green eyes. "This damn hammock should carry a warning stating that making love in it can be hazardous to your health."

"Is that what we were going to do?" she asked, a little shyly.

"The thought had crossed my mind," he said with a touch of dry humor. "In fact, I think about making love to you quite often. I'm becoming impatient to make my fantasy real, but never in my wildest imaginings have we ever been in a hammock."

She smiled. "And here I thought you were the one who liked a challenge," she teased.

"A challenge is one thing, but a circus act is something else."

She laughed. "I don't see any exit signs or parachutes, so how do we get out of this thing?"

"Like this." Lifting her up into his arms, he swung his legs out of the hammock and onto the ground, carrying her easily.

Her arms had gone around his neck for balance. "My hero."

"You betcha."

"You can put me down now. We're on solid ground."

He looked thoughtful. "I'm debating."

"About what? It's real easy. You let go of my legs and I'm standing on my own two bare feet."

"I'm debating about putting you down."

"Or what?"

"Or not putting you down."

"You are the most maddening man I've ever met." She crossed her arms over her chest, tying to look as severe as possible while feeling completely ridiculous. "I insist that you put me down."

"Yes, ma'am." He obeyed, but with a roguish smile. Once she was standing in front of him, he asked. "Do you want to take your clothes off here or in the cabin?"

"*What*?"

He laughed. "Abby, what an interesting mind you have. Unless you want to get your clothes wet, you have to remove them before you go swimming. You have your bathing suit on underneath, don't you?"

Taking a page out of his book on how to be provoking, she sauntered down to the shore without answering his question. Looking out over the water, she slipped off her knit top, then her shorts, dropping them on the dry sand. Her swimsuit was a rather respectable bikini that covered enough of her to be decent, but she still felt exposed and vulnerable. She took several steps into the water, then dove under the surface, emerging farther out.

Webb didn't move until he saw her head turn and her eyes find him. Then he began to strip off his clothes, taking his time. The simple act of undressing with Abby watching him was unbelievably arousing, almost as exciting as watching her a moment ago.

When he unsnapped his jeans, Abby came out of her trance and began swimming toward the wooden raft. The cold water felt like liquid ice on her heated skin. Today was for hoarding memories, but she doubted if her mind could conjure up the way the sun glazed Webb's tanned skin, highlighting his muscular chest. He was marvelously built, a stunning example of masculinity, and . . . and he was taking his pants off.

It was this last, salient fact that had caused her to head for the raft. She boosted herself up on it and sat on the edge, her feet dangling in the water.

In a short time, Webb's powerful strokes had brought him to the raft as well. He held on to its edge and looked up at her.

The sun was in his eyes, and he squinted. "You may not have learned to fish," he said, "but you certainly can swim when a man is taking his pants off."

He flattened both palms on the raft and was about to pull himself up to it when she stopped him.

"You aren't getting out of the water," she said emphatically.

He paused, slanting a look in her direction. "Why not?"

"For fear of sounding like a prude, do you have a bathing suit on?"

He smiled, a devilish smile. "If you hadn't been in such a rush, you would have known the answer to that question."

"Well?"

"Does it make that much difference if I don't have a suit on? This is a private cove. No one ever comes here."

"There's always a first time. Some sweet little old lady could come paddling by in her canoe, see you in the buff and have a heart attack."

"Not if she's like Maudie. Your sweet little old neighbor would probably caution me about getting sunburned and carry on."

Abby had to concede the point, admitting Maudie was relatively shock-proof. The problem was, she wasn't.

Webb watched the emotions flit across Abby's expressive face. Sunlight glistened on her wet skin and slicked-back hair. Her eyes reflected the light off the water, giving them a brilliance a man could lose himself in. He wanted to be that man.

He brushed her leg as he rested both arms on the raft. "I can't stay in the water forever, you know."

She shrugged, pretending a nonchalance she wasn't feeling. "It's your raft."

In a single, lithe movement, he propelled himself up beside her, giving her a clear view of black swimming trunks and muscular thighs.

Abby hoped her relief didn't show. Sounding casual about his nudity was easier than being confronted with it.

"I'm curious," he said. "What would you have done if I had forgotten my swimming trunks?"

Her mouth eased into a self-conscious smile. "I don't know. Probably made some stupid witty remark and looked up at the sky a lot."

He trailed a finger down her spine, feeling an involuntary tremor run along her skin. "Our reactions are quite different. I don't find the idea of you without clothing remotely funny." His fingers had stopped at the fastener of her top. "And I wouldn't look away."

She searched his eyes, and her lips parted in surprise when she read the expression there.

Webb didn't bother to hide his desire. It simmered in the gray depths of his eyes and skimmed around his sensual mouth. There was an electric current flowing through his fingers wherever he touched her.

Finding it suddenly difficult to breathe, she whispered, "What would you do?"

"Let's find out."

The clasp of her top was released as he gently pressed her back onto the sun-warmed deck. He eased the straps down her arms and removed the top. His eyes caressed her, making her skin tingle. "You are more beautiful than I imagined."

"I wish you'd stop saying that," she said quietly.

He tore his gaze away from her body to stare into her eyes. What he saw stunned him. She didn't believe him! "Abby, you are the most beautiful woman I've ever met." His hand stroked across her rib cage. "It seems like I've wanted you forever."

Her eyes closed so she could savor the sweet agony of his hand on her breast.

"Open your eyes, Abby. Look at me."

She obeyed, opening her eyes to look into his, losing herself in the smoky depths. Her breathing quickened as his hand caressed and kneaded her sensitive flesh.

"I'm not looking away," he murmured huskily. "I'm not strong enough to deny myself the pleasure of looking at you."

Gazing down at her, Webb was entranced. Her eyes spoke volumes, of desire, of surrender, of passion, and of pleasure. Yet even now there was an elusive quality about her. A mounting tenderness blended with a primitive urge to make this woman his own, to stake a claim on her mind and body.

"Abby," he groaned against her parted lips. "You take my breath away."

His mouth covered hers. She knew she wasn't beautiful, but as his tongue invaded her moist mouth with unleashed hunger, she felt attractive and desirable. Her senses were reeling from the exquisite pressure of his bare chest on her breasts.

Feeling as though he would explode, Webb tried to slow his raging desire. She deserved whatever control he could find.

He broke away from her mouth to taste and tease her vulnerable neck. "Abby, if you want me to stop, you'd better tell me now."

"No," she said breathlessly, her fingers weaving through his hair. "I know what I'm doing." She was making memories, and they would have to last her a long time.

His hands slid under her, bringing her hips against his aching body. A wave of pleasure swept over her, cresting as his strong fingers slid under the remaining scrap of fabric. She caught her breath, wanting him to end the torment his touch was creating deep inside her. The world as she knew it had vanished. There was only the two of them and the burning demands of their bodies.

"Abby," he said, his voice raspy. "I didn't plan for this to happen. I'm not prepared."

He began to draw back from her, and she panicked. Her arms tightened around him. "It's all right."

And it was. She couldn't think of anything more wonderful than conceiving Webb's child. Considering her own circumstances of birth, she was amazed she was thinking that way, but having Webb's child would be even more glorious than adopting one.

He was still trying to give her one last chance to change her mind. "Are you sure?"

"Yes." Her hands dove into his hair to bring his head back down to her.

"Ah, Abby," he breathed against her mouth. "I have to make you mine. I'm aching for you."

Webb felt the restless arch of her hips and her total surrender as he claimed her mouth. He had wanted a woman before, but never like this. Nothing was like this.

She clung to him as his swimming trunks were swept away, the last barrier removed between them. Even lost in passion, he thought of her comfort and slid his hands under her, cushioning her from the hard surface of the raft.

She cried out, not recognizing her own voice, as her body accepted his totally, desperately. Her body became like a violin, its strings stretched tightly as they vibrated with exquisitely sweet music.

Finally she had someone of her own, at least for a little while. Webb was hers right now, and it was enough.

Clinging to him tightly, she felt as though she would shatter into a million pieces and then she did just that as he arched against her one final time. His mouth captured her cry of release, even as he moaned from the intense pleasure that flooded through him.

For a long time, he held her while their hearts slowly returned to normal, then he shifted off her, bringing her with him as he rolled onto his back.

His hands reached up to frame her face. "I'm going to have this raft bronzed."

His unexpected remark made her laugh. "That fond of it, are you?"

The pressure of his hands brought her head down.

He met her halfway, kissing her thoroughly. "I am now." His hand swept down over her back and hips. "Are you all right? This raft isn't exactly a feather bed."

"I'm fine." She was more than fine. She had never felt more alive in her life.

His fingers trailed across the delicate bones of her face. "You're a special lady, Abby," he said seriously. "My lady. I might as well make that clear now. Is that going to be a problem for you?"

It was a speedy drop back to earth and reality. "It depends on what being your lady means."

"It means you and me. Together. I won't share you with anyone else. It means weekends here at the cabin or my place or yours and seeing each other whenever we can during the week."

"Let's not talk about tomorrow."

He could feel her withdrawing even though she hadn't moved.

"Why not?"

She sat up abruptly and reached for the scraps of material lying on the raft. "We have today," she said as she slipped her bathing suit on. "That has to be enough."

Webb wouldn't accept that, but before he could argue the point, Abby had dived headfirst into the water and was heading for the shore.

Seven

Webb caught up with her just as she was wading ashore. He grabbed her arm in a grip of steel and yanked her around to face him.

"It's not that easy, Abby," he said. "You can't just say today is all we have and then run away. Tell me what's going on in that peculiar mind of yours. What's wrong?"

"There's nothing wrong," she said. Despite the few seconds he had spent pulling on his bathing suit, he had still overtaken her. She had hoped to have a bit more time.

"The hell there isn't. One minute you're melting in my arms and the next you're pushing me away. I want to know why."

"Don't ruin what's left of today, Webb."

There was a pleading quality in her voice that hurt him. He relaxed his hold on her some, but still held her firmly enough to keep her from moving away from him. "I'm not the one spouting off about there being only today. What's wrong with having a to-morrow?"

"You know what my schedule is like. I don't have time to be involved with anyone right now. I barely have time for myself. I can't give you what you want."

"You haven't a clue as to what I want."

"You want tomorrows. I can't give them to you."

"You gave me your body out on that raft. What was that? A farewell gesture?"

She flinched, incredibly hurt. Fists of tension tightened her stomach, making her feel slightly sick. "I hadn't planned for that to happen."

Webb knew he had hurt her, but he was hurting too. Damn, he wished he could understand her. "But you did plan to say good-bye at the end of the day, didn't you? You allotted one day out of your hectic, precious schedule to spend with me, and then you planned to go back to your work without any thought of how I might feel about being used. I'm not a toy you can pick up, play with, and then discard."

The color drained from her face. He was right. She hadn't thought about his feelings. He was also right about her allowing herself the one day with him.

"I didn't set out to use you," she said in a voice trembling with emotion. "It may look that way, but it's not true."

"Maybe I could believe you if you explained why we only have today." He held up his hand when she was about to speak. "I don't want to hear about your backbreaking schedule. I already know about that. I want to know why we can't work around it. I work, too, Abby, but I've made room for you."

Averting her eyes, she said, "You're making this very difficult."

"You're damn right I am. I'm trying to make you

see it's impossible to give me your laughter, your smiles, and your body one day, then expect me to go along with a polite dismissal at the end of that day." He took several angry steps away from her before turning back. "My God, Abby, how can you say there will be no tomorrows for us after what happened between us today?"

Like a cornered animal, Abby attacked in defense of herself. "Have you ever wanted something so badly, you're willing to mortgage your soul, knowing you will have to pay later? That's how badly I wanted to spend today with you. I can't remember the last time I put everything else aside, like I have today." She looked out over the water. "I won't be able to do it again."

"Why? What is so important that you can't take any more time off for yourself?"

"I have to finish my thesis. I have to get my master's."

Webb searched her face for a long moment. Repeating her reply several times in his head didn't make anything any clearer. She had to finish her thesis. That was what she said. Her master's degree. Why did getting her degree mean she couldn't see him any more?

"I don't remember saying you have to give up your work on your thesis in order to spend time with me. There's such a thing as compromise. I know getting your degree is important to you, but I don't understand why you have to exclude me from your life in order to obtain it."

"You just said the magic word. Time. It's something I don't have a lot of, and I won't until I finish the thesis. I have to work to support myself and to pay back the loan for my tuition. That takes up a lot of hours, a lot of time away from working on the thesis."

Webb saw the strain in her face and the rigid way she was standing. It wasn't easy for her to open up to him. He had the feeling she still wasn't telling him everything, but she had given him something to go on. Abby was like a complicated maze. He kept turning corners, only to be blocked by a barrier of her pride, her independence, or just plain stubbornness. Somehow he would find the way through to her.

When he didn't say anything, Abby walked to where she had left her clothes on the sand. She slipped them on over her damp bikini. When Webb still remained silent, she looked at him. "Are we going back now?"

He seemed to be preoccupied, staring off into space. She repeated her question, and he finally heard her. "We might as well," he said quietly.

The drive back was made in silence. Abby wished she knew what Webb was thinking. His expression was unreadable and he kept his attention on the road. She sat huddled against the door, feeling miserable even as she kept telling herself she had done the right thing. Her childhood had taught her not to expect much from life unless it came from the sweat of her brow. Nothing in her past had prepared her for someone like Webb. He had given her so much, and she had gloried in his company, his laughter, his teasing. And finally she had selfishly taken him into her body to experience the joyous pleasure of belonging to someone completely. She had greedily grabbed a chance to be with him for one day, and now he was demanding more.

When he stopped the truck in front of her house, she didn't expect him to get out. But when did he ever do anything she expected? He walked beside her to the door, waving casually to Maudie, who was sweeping off her front porch. He took the house key out of her hand and gently pushed her inside after he'd unlocked the door. On his way into the living room, he dropped the keys onto a small table in the hallway.

Abby bit her lip as she slowly followed him. Why was he staying?

"Sit down, Abby," he said. "There's something I want to discuss with you."

Her shoulders slumped wearily. "There's nothing left to discuss. I've told you it's over. Why can't you accept that?"

When she didn't move, Webb took her arm and pulled her toward the sofa. He sat her down, then joined her.

"You still don't get it, do you?" he said, his fingers playing with a lock of her hair, "You're so used to charging ahead alone, you can't imagine having anyone help you fight your dragons." He looked very satisfied with himself. "I'm volunteering to be your dragon slayer. While I was driving back here, I figured out how to solve both our problems. I want to continue to see you, but you feel you don't have the time to spare to be with me because you have to work. Right?"

She nodded cautiously.

"The solution is simple. I'll pay off your loan and take care of your expenses so you won't have to work. You can spend more hours finishing your thesis and studying, and still have time to be with me."

"No." She stood up and quickly crossed the room. "I won't take money from you. I already owe you for fixing the roof and for four new tires."

He had expected her to refuse. "It's not a question of taking it. All you have to do is accept it, as you would a gift."

"It's charity no matter how you wrap it," she argued. "I've gotten this far without having to pass the hat, thank you very much. I've found that gifts usually come with a tag, an obligation. What's the tag on your offer, Webb? Would you expect something in exchange for keeping me? I'm not good mistress material."

He fought an instant surge of fury. If he was to fight off her dragons, he needed a stronger weapon than anger. "You don't have much faith in mankind, do you?" he said, then changed direction. "What happens after you get your degree?"

It took her a few seconds to make the shift. It was an innocent enough question, but she was guarded with her reply. "I've been offered a job as an instructor at the university once I get my master's."

"Is that what you want?"

Avoiding his sharp gaze, she lifted her chin. "Yes."

He didn't believe her. "Let me put it another way. Is that all you want?"

Her eyes met his, and she couldn't keep the sadness from her expression. She wanted it all: love, marriage, a home, children, a career. She wanted too much. Settling for what she could have, financial security and a child of her own, would be enough.

She repeated her earlier answer, this time in a quieter voice. "Yes."

"Then let me help you get it."

His soft-spoken request was tempting. It would mean she could get off the merry-go-round she was on and live a fairly normal existence. Still, she knew she would turn him down. Her pride wouldn't let her do anything else. Even so, it was surprisingly difficult to reject his offer. "I appreciate the fact that you want to help, but I have to do it myself."

There was a sudden knocking on the back door. Abby knew immediately who it was. Maudie and Ira were the only people who came to that door, and Maudie knew Webb was here.

She walked into the kitchen to answer the door, leaving Webb alone in the living room. Whatever Maudie had to say, she didn't want Webb to hear it. Like Webb, Maudie took a lot for granted about their relationship.

It wasn't Maudie. It was Ira, and he had an invitation to extend to her and Webb. "Maudie was hoping you and your young man could come share dinner with us. It won't be much, just common, everyday fare, but there's plenty." Which meant Maudie had headed for the kitchen the minute she saw Webb, Abby thought. The table would be groaning under the weight of an astonishing array of "common, everyday fare."

As she was about to decline, a voice behind her accepted. Turning her head, she saw Webb striding toward her. She stiffened when he casually put his arm around her shoulders.

"If you don't mind taking us the way we are," he said, "we'd love to come to dinner with you and Maudie."

Ira shook his head. "We ain't fancy folks. You been on a picnic?"

"And fishing. What time would you like us to be there?"

Ira beamed at them. "Dinner will be ready in about an hour, but you can come over anytime. I have some dandelion wine you might like to sample before dinner."

Webb nodded. "Give us a few minutes to clean up a little and we'll be over. Can we bring anything?"

"Just yourselves." Ira was grinning broadly as he went down the back steps. Those two youngsters looked so perfect together, he thought. This was going to make Maudie's day. Maybe he had better get out two bottles of wine just in case.

While Ira was feeling very pleased with himself, Abby was glaring at Webb. "Are you crazy? Why did you agree to have dinner with them? Do you have any idea what you're in for?" Her voice was raised several decibels. "Haven't you heard one word I've said in the last hour?"

"Is this multiple choice or essay?" he asked, smiling down at her, not taking her outrage seriously.

He defeated her at every turn, she thought in dismay. "What am I going to do with you?" she murmured soberly, leaning her forehead against his chest as he turned her in his arms. "You don't take seriously a single word I say. I'm trying to do the right thing and you don't pay any attention to me."

His hands rested on her shoulders, gently easing her back so she could look up at him. "Honey, I've heard every word you've ever said to me. I just don't necessarily agree with everything you say." He leaned down and brushed his mouth across hers. "It comes down to, you know what you want and I know what I want. I believe we want the same things. We just have different ways of getting them. It's really very simple. You make it appear complicated."

She shook her head. "You baffle me. You really do."

His smile melted her bones. "You have to learn to trust someone other than yourself. It will all work out. You'll see." The last thing he wanted to do was be with other people right now. All he wanted was to taste and touch Abby. "We have some dandelion wine waiting for us next door."

She glanced down at her bare legs. "I'll go change."

While she dressed in a khaki poplin skirt and crisp white blouse, Abby attempted to analyze the results of her discussion with Webb. Nothing seemed to have been resolved at all. Webb was like one of his bulldozers, impervious to any obstacle, mowing down everything in his path. She only wished she knew what his destination was.

The evening with Maudie and Ira was an experience in stuffing themselves silly. Maudie wasn't satisfied until they each had at least a second helping of every dish, considering it a personal affront if they declined. While Maudie was pushing the food, Ira was busy pouring dandelion wine into their glasses every time they took a swallow.

"Now, I know it's not much, but do the best you can," Maudie said more than once as she handed around a platter of roast beef, followed by a dish of fried chicken.

Maudie had a lot in common with Noah, Abby had discovered. She believed all types of food should come in twos: two kinds of meat, two different vegetables, two salads, and two scrumptious desserts.

Abby had warned Webb beforehand to take small portions each time and to go easy on Ira's lethal homemade wine. When it came to Maudie's probing questions, he was on his own. To Abby's surprise, Maudie acted relatively harmless and congenial. Instead of pouncing on Webb, using interrogation techniques perfected over the years, she aimed only a few direct shots at Webb, which he skillfully deflected.

Mostly Maudie spent the evening giving a glowing

account of Abby's many talents. She worked in what a great cook Abby was when Webb complimented the dinner. Each time she could, she found some way to praise Abby, even if she had to stretch the subject to fit the testimonial.

Several hours later, Abby and Webb said good night to their hosts and walked back to Abby's house. It was a lovely night, with a bright moon lighting their way.

"I thought you were exaggerating," Webb said, "when you warned me about Ira's wine. I think it dissolved the fillings in my teeth."

"I would never kid about something as powerful as Ira's wine." She inhaled the fresh night air, hoping to dilute the effects of the wine. "They don't mean any harm by shoving me down your throat the way they do."

"They're very fond of you."

By this time they had reached the back door of her house. Abby sank down on the steps. "I know." Leaning back against the door, she looked up at the moon. "This air feels good. A little of Ira's wine goes a long way."

Webb's shoulder brushed hers as he joined her on the step. "They seem to be charter members of the Abigil Stout fan club, and want me to join."

She sighed. "Sorry about that. Maudie means well. She's somewhat old-fashioned and doesn't realize how things are."

He studied her. The moonlight lay gently on her hair and highlighted the delicate bones of her face. "And how are things?" he asked.

Suddenly weary, she closed her eyes. "Maudie believes if a man and a woman spend some time together, it's happily-ever-after time. She isn't aware of how temporary most relationships are. Ever since I moved in next door, she and Ira have tried to convince me that the answer to all my problems is hearth, home, and hero. They think my life is unnatural if I don't have someone to share it with." She smiled faintly, opening her eyes. "Maudie's idea of woman's liberation is going without her girdle."

As Webb considered Abby's reply, one of her comments struck him. It was as though a light had flashed on in his mind, illuminating a blurred impression, bringing it into focus. "That's it," he muttered under his breath. "That's got to be it."

Wondering what in the world had come over him, Abby frowned and asked, "What's wrong with you? If you've got a roblem because of Ira's wine, I don't have the antidote."

His eyes drilled into hers as he weighed the pros and cons of his theory. "It's not your degree that's the problem."

"It's not?"

"Oh, it's part of it, but there's more."

"There is?"

He slapped his palms against his thighs, then charged to his feet to pace the ground in front of the steps. "You have to do everything yourself because you don't trust anyone else to stick around. All you've ever had were temporary homes, temporary parents, temporary relationships. You expect people to walk away eventually, don't you?"

He stopped in front of her, leaning down to peer into her wide, startled eyes. "You expect me to wander off one of these days, too, so you're giving me my walking papers first. I'm right, aren't I?"

She ducked away from him, sliding off the step to stand on the grass. "I'm a realist."

"Is that what you call it? I would think 'coward'

would be a better word." His hands were on his hips in his usual angry, aggressive stance. "How do you know what I'm going to do? Hell, since I've met you, I don't know what I'm going to do half the time, so how can you possibly know? I may have more staying power than you think."

"To give you an example of your staying power," she said, her own anger rising, "how about the night you asked me to have dinner with you? When I said no, you promptly found a replacement, the blonde with the sprayed-on white dress. Then you took her home and later decided to come back to the hotel because you were curious about why I'd turned down a chance to spend an evening with you." Her chin went up. "Tell me I'm wrong. Tell me it didn't happen that way. Tell me I'm not a novelty you'll get out of your system in time and then move on."

"You have it all figured out. You think you know me so well." He crossed his arms over his chest to keep from grabbing her and giving her the shaking of her life. The fact that she had been fairly accurate didn't make it any easier for him to defend her accusation. "How do you explain what happened between us on the raft? Internal combustion? Chemical imbalance? Sunstroke?"

His sarcasm bit into her like the lashing of a whip, cutting deep. Her voice sounded as if it came from far away, and her words held a strange hollowness. "How you felt inside me will be a part of my memory for a long time, probably forever. Now, if you will excuse me," she added with dignity, "I am going to bed."

Webb stayed rooted to the spot, his gaze remaining on the door Abby had closed quietly after her. His arms dropped to his sides and he took a deep breath, feeling as if he had just been punched in the stomach.

He stared at the dark windows of the house, wondering why she wasn't turning on any lights. Was she crying? Lord, he hoped not. Damn, she had him so tied up in knots, he was never going to get free.

It was going to take one gigantic teddy bear to get him back in her good graces this time.

Eight

During the next several days, Abby was again caught up in her whirlwind schedule. If she was a little quieter than usual, somewhat preoccupied, no one mentioned it to her. She did her work diligently, if somewhat automatically and without her usual enthusiasm.

When she arrived home from the hotel each night, there was a new teddy bear to add to the collection on her dresser. Every night a different stuffed bear would be waiting at her piano for her. There was never any note, and no one ever saw who put them there. Each night she held the bear as she drove home. Each night she lay in bed staring at the ceiling, unable to sleep, and occasionally her gaze drifted over to the silent reminders of Webb Hunter.

Everything became a struggle. It was easier to skip meals than to fix something to eat. The few hours of sleep she managed to get were haunted by dreams of what might have been if circumstances had been different, if she had been different.

She placed the blame for the way things had turned

out squarely where she felt it belonged—on herself. She had known Webb wouldn't stick around long. Nobody had before. Why should he be any different? That he had accurately surmised how she felt had surprised her. It was an insight she hadn't considered in so many words, and it was disturbing that Webb had found the words.

By Thursday she was edgy, jumping at sudden noises, having difficulty concentrating on her work. Her head was filled with the familiar low buzzing sound caused by lack of sleep. She made several errors about dates while showing people around Bristol House, forgot where she had parked her car at the supermarket, and once nearly fell asleep in her driveway after she had shut off the engine.

And that was another thing. Her car. It was a reminder of Webb and the repair debt she owed. But then, everything seemed to remind her of Webb. Her newly repaired porch roof, a coffee mug in her kitchen, even fish displayed at the super market conjured thoughts of Webb when she least expected them.

As she got ready for work Thursday evening, Abby chose one of her favorite dresses, an ivory-colored georgette one that was flattering and comfortable, a rare combination in evening wear. The blouson top was decorated with ivory lace across the shoulders, around the stand-up collar, and on the wide cuffs. The full skirt flowed gracefully, swishing softly when she moved. She took extra pains with her makeup to repair the ravages of sleepless nights. Her freshly washed hair was piled on top of her head, exposing her slender neck. She knew her appearance would pass the strict code of dress the lounge manager insisted on, but she could only stare at the mirrored image of herself, wondering about the woman behind the makeup.

She knew her reflection was deceptive. There was no sign of the lonely child within, the child Webb had seen and pointed out to her. At first she had been shocked and hurt by his sharp perception. Then she had resented it. Who was he to analyze and dissect her, to criticize the way she lived her life? Unless he had been there, handed from one family to another like a book from the library, never knowing where he was going to live or for how long, he had no right to judge how she lived.

During a tour at Bristol House that day, Abby had seen another side of the coin of life. A teenage brother and sister had accompanied their parents on the tour, clearly unhappy with their parents' choice of entertainment. They had bickered until their father had ordered them to go to the car, since they couldn't behave properly. As the teenagers had passed Abby, she'd overheard the girl grumble, "Mary Lou's lucky. Her parents never drag her anywhere."

The girl's comment had made Abby wonder if Mary Lou's complaint might be that her parents never took her anywhere.

It boiled down to individuals' interpretations of the way they had been treated, she thought now. All people probably had some regrets about incidents in their childhoods and wished that circumstances had been different, without realizing that different circumstances might not necessarily have been better.

The solution was to get on with it. Play the cards dealt out, gamble with a good hand, and throw in a bad one. The main thing was to keep playing.

Her gaze shifted from her reflection to the stuffed bears on the dresser. Webb had brought teddy bears to that inner child, acknowledging the child in all adults who receive pleasure from simple things. His amusement when Maudie had purchased a stuffed goose for her elderly husband had been genuine, not ridiculing. Webb himself had shown her his playful side at the lake with his newest toy, the hammock.

But she knew that wasn't the type of child he had referred to on Sunday night. The insecurity of her childhood had carried over into her adult life, affecting her judgment. It was this child who needed to grow up.

Another teddy bear was waiting for her at the piano. This one was dressed in bib overalls, and a miniature set of workman's tools hung from a belt around his pudgy waist. A baseball cap was perched between his ears, and the initials H C had been printed on it with a felt-tip pen. Hunter Construction had also been printed across the bib.

From a dark corner on the other side of the lounge, Webb saw Abby's mouth curve slightly in a sad smile as she traced the lettering with her finger. At least she hadn't thrown the bear across the room, he thought. A waiter approached his table, and Webb ordered a soda. It was going to be another long night.

At about midnight, Abby returned to the piano, after a brief break, to find a group of businessmen pulling several tables together. Neckties were loosened, drinks were ordered in pairs, and cigar and cigarette smoke hovered over the tables. Then the requests came. It seemed every man there had a wife or girlfriend whose name was a song title. Next came songs about their home states. Next came the inevitable sing-a-long.

By the time the bar was closing, Abby's fingers were stiff as they moved over the keys, automatically finding the notes for "Good night, Ladies." When she was finished she tucked the teddy bear into the crook of her arm, and retrieved her shawl and purse from the employees' lounge, not particularly caring if anyone saw her carrying a stuffed animal. Her footsteps were muffled by the thick gray carpet as she walked through the lobby, each step an effort, as though her delicate high-heeled sandals were made of lead.

The fresh, early-morning air hit her as soon as she pushed open the thick glass doors, and she pulled her shawl more tightly around her.

It was a policy of the hotel for all female employees to be escorted to their cars after dark, but the security guard was nowhere in sight. The doorman was attending to the luggage of a late arrival, so Abby waited by the entrance. She wasn't sure she had the energy to make it to her car at the moment anyway.

Closing her eyes, she leaned back against the building. Another long day was almost over, and now an even longer night would begin. Although she was weary to the bone, she was in no hurry to go home to stare at the ceiling with teddy bears as her only company.

A strong hand closed over her arm, but she wasn't too concerned. She thought it was the doorman.

"Come on, Abby. I'm taking you home."

Her eyes flew open. "Webb? What are you doing here?"

A muscle jerked in his jaw. Damn, he thought. She looked more exhausted than ever. "I'm taking you home."

The doorman came toward them, his expression guarded. "Miss Stout? Are you all right?"

"Yes, I'm fine, Ralph."

"Do you know this man?"

She looked at Webb for a long moment, then finally said, "Yes."

"Do you want me to walk you to your car now?" the doorman asked.

Webb answered for her. "I'll take care of her."

The doorman wasn't about to take the stranger's word for it. "Miss Stout?"

She wasn't up to arguing with either one of them. "Mr. Hunter will walk me to my car, Ralph. It's all right. I'll be fine. See you tomorrow night."

The doorman obviously still wasn't convinced, and he watched as Webb took Abby's arm and guided her toward the parking lot. Instead of heading toward her car, though, he led her to his.

"Mr. Hunter will drive you home," he drawled. "You can barely walk, much less drive a car."

Abby didn't argue. He was here. That was all she wanted to think about right now. Not why he was here or for how long. She got in the car and closed her eyes as she leaned her head back. He was with her. That was enough for now. Ironically, she wasn't able to enjoy his company. She fell asleep.

When he reached her house Webb lifted her from the car and carried her up her front steps, careful not to wake her. After a few seconds of fumbling for the lock with the key he had taken out of her purse, he pushed open the door. Her face was buried against his neck, her body relaxed in sleep. He flicked on a light switch with his elbow and strode down the hall in search of her bedroom.

The first door he came to was slightly ajar, and he pushed it open with his foot. The light from the hall illuminated the dark interior enough for him to see this was not her bedroom. His eyes narrowed as he stared at the contents of the room. There was a small white dresser, a rocking chair painted white, and . . . a crib. A baby crib, also painted white. Webb could only stand in the doorway holding the sleeping woman, unable to believe what he was seeing.

Slowly he backed out into the hall and walked to the other door. This was Abby's bedroom. He pulled back the old quilt cover and laid her down on the double bed. His gaze wandered around the room, finding the stuffed bears assembled on an old oak dresser. It was the only other piece of furniture, except for the bed and a nightstand. This room was like a nun's cell, compared to the cheerful furnishings in the other room.

He looked down at Abby. What in the hell was going on? Was she pregnant? A variety of thoughts raced through his mind, none of them pleasant and all of them having to do with the furniture in the other room. Had she baited the age-old trap of being pregnant by another man and setting him up to take the fall? He remembered the flat plane of her stomach that his hands had caressed. If she was pregnant, she wasn't showing yet.

His eyes were narrow slits as he examined every inch of her face, as though the answers would be found there. Her long lashes rested on her cheeks, and her lips were slightly parted. Looking at her now, vulnerable and lovely in sleep, he couldn't believe she would use him like that. There had to be some other, logical reason why she would have baby furniture in her home. That room had been fixed up with more loving care than her own room.

Hating to wake her when she needed sleep so badly, he sat down on the edge of the bed and began to shake her gently. He had to know now. Thinking about the reason a single woman would set up a room for a baby was making him crazy. His imagination was coming up with too many variables, none of them to his liking. It was three in the morning, not the best time for a little chat, but he wanted the truth.

"Abby. Wake up."

Abby fought a tug of war. Her conscious mind was nudging her awake and her tired body wanted sleep. A warm hand stroked her cheek, pulling her further out of the depths of sleep. Her heavy lids opened enough to see the shadowy figure leaning over her.

"Hi," she said drowsily. "You're in my dreams again."

Webb let his hand fall away from her. This was no dream, he thought. It was a bloody damn nightmare. He reached over to the nightstand and turned on the small bedside lamp.

"Abby, we need to talk."

The light hurt her eyes, and she squinted at him. "I'm so tired, Webb. I don't want to talk." She started to roll away from him onto her side.

His hands closed over her narrow shoulders, and he pulled her up into a sitting position, facing him. His voice cut through the stillness of the night. "It has to be now, Abby. You have some explaining to do."

The harsh, gritty tone of his voice and the hard fingers digging into her cleared the fog of sleep, and she looked up at him, startled. What in tarnation was wrong with him now? "About what?"

The coil of hair on the top of her head had been loosened, and the abundant mass was tumbling down over her shoulders. Her stunning eyes were heavy with sleep. He forced his mind away from how desirable she looked and concentrated on the reason he had wakened her.

"Abby, tell me I'm wrong. Tell me I haven't been chosen to take the blame for the baby."

She frowned in confusion and was barely able to pronounce the word. "Baby? What baby?"

"The one the furniture in the other room is for. The baby can't be mine unless you ran out and got that furniture in the last two days and know something I don't know." He jerked his hands away from her and stood up. "That trick is as old as the hills, Abby, but men keep falling for it. When were you going to give me the news? After we had made love a few more times? Were you going to wait a month or so before you sprang it on me?"

All the blood seemed to flow out of her body, leaving her cold and drained. Slowly she slid back until she met the headboard. Her dress rustling softly, she drew her knees up to her chest and wrapped her arms tightly around her legs. As the meaning of his words finally sank in, she stared at him in disbelief.

"I'm not pregnant," she said in a choked voice.

"Then why the baby furniture?"

Now she understood what he was talking about. "It's none of your business."

His hands were on his hips. "Last Sunday it became my business."

She looked away, not wanting him to see the pain in her eyes. "I am responsible for my own actions, including what happened on the raft. I don't remember asking for anything from you afterward."

"Why the baby furniture?"

She laid her forehead against her knees for a long moment. This really wasn't happening, she thought. This would all be a dim memory when she woke in the morning. The burning sensation in her eyes reminded her she was awake. Taking a deep breath, she raised her head and looked up at him.

"If I answer your question, will you leave?" Her voice was harsh with suppressed pain. "And never come back?"

"You aren't in a position to make conditions, Abby. Answer the question."

She stared at the wall opposite the bed. "It's funny," she said as if talking to herself. "I thought I had everything figured out today." Lowering her legs, she smoothed out her wrinkled dress before placing her clenched hands in her lap. Staring down, she began to tell her story, knowing he wouldn't leave until he'd heard it.

Leaving out her hopes and dreams and the years of working toward her goal, she starkly gave him the facts. "Once I get my master's degree, I will be able to meet the last requirement for adopting a baby. I'll be able to get a job with a decent salary. A social worker outlined what I had to have before I could qualify to adopt. A room set up for a baby is one of the requirements. Financial security is another. Strange as it may seem, a man isn't."

She looked up and saw his stunned expression. "That's it. Sorry to disappoint you. There's no great devious plot to use you as a stud so I can have a child of my own. I'd been planning to adopt a child long before I ever met you, so you're off the hook."

Webb sank down onto the bed, aware that she drew her feet away from him. Dammit, was he ever going to stop making wrong assumptions about her? Ever going to stop hurting her?

"Abby . . ." he began haltingly.

"I want you to leave, Webb. You now know my deep, dark secret and I've reassured you that you have nothing to worry about. That's all there is. There's nothing left. You've taken it all." If she had managed to conceive a child when they had made love, he would never know about it.

The slight tremor in her voice made him look at her. Her eyes were shiny with unshed tears, her chin lifted proudly, defiantly. The expression in her eyes tore at his insides, tightening his chest, making him feel like the lowest thing on earth.

While he watched, a single tear slowly slid down her pale cheek, and claws of guilt clamped around his heart.

He reached for her, ignoring the way she resisted and tried to evade him. "No, don't pull away. I won't hurt you."

The moment his arms enfolded her against his warm body, her tears fell in earnest. He eased her down onto the bed and held her, wishing he could somehow erase the pain he had inflicted on her.

"I'm sorry, Abby. I know it's inadequate to say, but it's true. You can't be calling me any names I'm not already calling myself. Some dragon slayer I turned out to be."

In spite of her own pain, she was able to see his. "Perhaps you should retire from the field," she said. Her voice was hoarse from exhaustion and emotion.

His lips caressed her face, his tongue finding the tears. "I can't do that. I'll do anything in the world for you, but not that. What I have to do is stop jumping to conclusions where you are concerned."

She took a shuddering breath, then sighed. "You jump to obvious conclusions. I don't suppose you come across baby furniture in a single woman's home every day."

"I can't say it's ever happened before." He rolled onto his back, bringing her with him, his arms keeping her close. Her head nestled on his shoulder. "Now I know what motivates you to carry the work load of three people. You want a child."

"Yes."

His fingers combed through her hair. "What's wrong with the old-fashioned way of getting a baby? It's worked for centuries."

"Your own reaction answers your question. Besides, there haven't been a lot of volunteers."

His hand stilled in her hair; then his fingers pulled gently to raise her head so he could see her face. "What if I volunteered?"

Her green eyes flared with anger. "That's not funny."

"I'm serious."

Pushing against his chest, she moved away from him. She pulled her dress out from under his leg and sat up. "A baby is the last thing you want to have anything to do with. You were horrified when you saw the furniture in the other room." She stood up and went to the closet, where she retrieved her robe from a hanger. "This is a stupid discussion. I'm going to take a shower. I don't expect you to be here when I get back."

He didn't move. He heard the click of the latch on the bathroom door and the sound of water flowing from the shower, but he stayed where he was. His own question had surprised him too. A child. Becoming a father was something he had never considered for himself, but the fantasy of having a child with Abby grew as the seconds ticked by.

If the urge to be a father had always been deep inside him, this was the first time it had surfaced. His brother's children had never sparked any latent paternal feelings, nor had he been jealous of Brad's having a family. His own, single lifestyle had suited him down to the ground. His freedom to come and go, to do as he liked when he liked, with whomever he liked, had been the way he wanted to live. Pipes, slippers, and the patter of little children's feet weren't for him . . . were they?

He swung his legs over the side of the bed and stood up. He had a lot of serious thinking to do.

* * *

Abby's gaze was drawn to the bed as she stood in the doorway of her room. Empty. It was ridiculous to feel disappointment, when she'd been the one to tell him to go.

She slipped off her robe, and pulled on her nightshirt. She brushed her hair, then crawled into bed. Taking a deep breath, she willed her body to relax, hoping to slip easily into the blessed oblivion of sleep. As exhaustion fogged her mind she reached out to turn off the lamp. At that moment, Webb walked calmly into the bedroom, holding a glass of milk.

Abby's mouth dropped open. "You left."

He lifted an eyebrow mockingly in response to her less-than-clever statement. "Sit up," he said as he walked over to the bed.

"Why?"

"Because it's easier to drink this sitting up than lying down."

"I don't want any milk." Nonetheless, she pulled herself up to lean against the headboard. "Why are you still here?"

He placed the glass in her hand, and the milk sloped dangerously near the rim. "Careful. It will do you more good if you drink it instead of wear it."

Giving him a look of irritation, she took a sip. "Do you realize what time it is?"

Shoving back his sleeve, he looked at his watch. "It's three thirty-three."

"*I* know what time it is. I wanted *you* to know what time it is. Are you aware of the fact that we just had a fight?"

He walked to the other side of the bed, kicked off his shoes, and lay down. His arms folded beneath his head, he casually crossed his legs at the ankles.

"But it's over. You know I don't stay mad long. Finish your milk."

He was going to drive her crazy. He really was. Stark, raving, tear-at-her-hair nuts. She looked down at him, her eyes scanning his long length sprawled out on the bed next to her. No man should look as compellingly male as he did. It just wasn't fair. "What do you think you're doing?"

Closing his eyes, he murmured, "Waiting for you to finish off that glass of milk. I would have fixed something more substantial, but your cupboards are bare, Mother Hubbard."

The glass was half empty when Abby thought of something that had bothered her earlier. "Webb?"

"Hmmm."

"Why were you at the hotel when I got off work?"

"To make sure you got home all right. A couple of those men had quite a lot to drink, and I wanted to make sure they weren't going to request something other than a song from you."

"You were in the lounge?"

"Hmmm." He didn't add that he had been there the last three nights, too.

Abby drained the glass and set it on the bedside table. Slanting a glance down at Webb, she let her gaze follow the lean lines of his body. She still found it hard to believe he was there beside her. So many unanswered questions were buzzing around in her head, but she wasn't up to asking any of them right now. Except for one.

"Webb?"

"Hmmm."

"Are you going to sleep?"

"Hmmm."

She wanted to touch his slightly mussed hair, so

dark against the plain white pillowcase. "You can't sleep here."

"It's too late. I'm already asleep." He opened his eyes enough to see if she had finished drinking the milk. Moving quickly for a man supposedly asleep, he slid an arm around her to bring her down beside him. Using the same tone of shocked indignation she had used earlier, he demanded, "Do you realize what time it is? Turn out the light."

Feeling an incredible desire to laugh, Abby gave in to the inevitable and turned off the lamp. He was going to get his way whether she argued or not. She didn't want to argue anyway. This was one of those time when life was handing her a gift. She wasn't going to refuse it. The *why*'s could wait.

Webb turned her so that her back was pressed against his chest, his arm coming to rest under her breasts. His voice rumbled softly against her neck. "What time is your class in the morning?"

"Nine."

"Okay."

She heard him release a long breath and felt his body relax against her. Her lashes lowered as she absorbed the warmth radiating from him, feeling unusually safe and secure.

A last, hazy thought filtered through her mind as she drifted off to sleep in his arms. Maybe, just maybe, this man was going to stick around after all.

Nine

The other side of the bed was empty when Abby opened her eyes at seven the next morning, making her wonder if she had been dreaming after all.

Rolling over onto her stomach, she buried her face in the other pillow. Her breath caught instantly, then she inhaled deeply. It hadn't been a dream. His scent remained on the pillow, reminding her of a sunny day on a lake, of strong arms and melting kisses, of exploring hands and shattering ecstasy.

Groaning aloud, she tossed back the covers and flung her legs over the edge of the bed. She tripped over part of the quilt and stumbled over to the dresser. As she pulled open the top drawer, something about one of the stuffed bears caught her attention. Beau, who stood beside the dresser, was holding a piece of white paper.

She removed the folded paper from the bear's paw. The sheet of ruled paper had been torn out of one of her notebooks. It read: "I'll be back at eight with your car." It was signed with his initial, and there was a postscript: "I was relieved to learn you don't snore, but I hate that thing you wear to bed."

Shaking her head, she sighed. He wore her out. Being with him was like trying to harness the wind. He swept in and out of her life, knocking her off-balance, leaving her exhausted yet exhilarated. It was impossible to keep up with him.

At eight o'clock sharp, there was a knock at her front door. She expected Webb to walk right in, since he apparently had her key ring, but when he rapped on the door again, she went to let him in. She smoothed her white cotton knit sweater down over her navy blue skirt as she approached the door.

When she opened it her smile of welcome faded, replaced by a puzzled frown. A tall man was standing on the porch holding a large bag in one hand. At first she couldn't figure out who he was, then she recognized him from the photos in Webb's office. His resemblance to Webb was startling. He was a few inches shorter and had a heavier build, but it was clear he and Webb were related. She correctly guessed this man was Webb's brother, Brad.

He smiled down at her. "Hi. Are you Abby?"

She returned the smile. "Yes."

"I'm Brad Hunter, Webb's brother. Webb will be here in a few minutes." He held up the bag. "I have breakfast."

She stepped aside. "Come in."

"I dropped Webb off at the hotel to pick up your car. I'm to wait here for him and drive him back to the office. I hope you don't mind me waiting for him with you. I could wait in the truck, but I wanted to meet you."

"I don't mind. There's coffee in the kitchen, if you'd like some."

While she poured coffee, Brad opened one cupboard after the other until he found a dinner plate. Like his brother, he immediately made himself at home, not expecting her to wait on him. From the bag he had brought with him, he took out an assortment of croissants, hot rolls, and frosted doughnuts and arranged them on the plate.

As he set the plate on the table he looked up at Abby. "My wife would have a fit. Can you believe it? She thinks this stuff is bad for you. She carries on about preservatives, monosodium glutomate, and hydrogenated whatevers, in tones of doom."

"Nothing that smells that good could possibly be bad for you."

"My sentiments exactly. Webb was right. You are one of a kind." The kitchen drawers were next on his search route.

Abby was a little taken aback by his last comment, not sure exactly what it meant. Still she couldn't help smiling at Brad, who had immediately taken over her kitchen, as his brother had done before. "What are you looking for?" she asked.

"A couple of knives and some butter."

"I'll get them for you."

He stopped her by pulling out the chair from the table and gently but forcibly pushing her into it. "You just sit tight. Point me in the right direction."

She pointed and he found what he was looking for. "You are definitely Webb's brother," she said, smiling.

His response was another broad smile. Once he had everything the way he wanted it, he pulled out the other chair and sat down.

"Webb said you needed your car this morning because you have a class to attend at the university. What are you taking?"

If Webb's brother thought it odd she hadn't driven her own car home, his face gave nothing away. "I'm taking a six-week refresher course on eighteenth-century domestic life. Today will be the last class."

His smile was warm and friendly, with a touch of curiosity. "I'm glad I finally get to meet the woman who has my big brother in a dither."

Abby felt her cheeks grow warm. "Not me," she said emphatically.

Helping himself to a cinnamon roll, Brad chuckled. "Since he isn't seeing anyone else but you, it looks like you are responsible for his strange behavior."

She hoped her surprise didn't show. Webb was seeing only her? "What would you consider strange behavior?"

Brad sipped his coffee, looking thoughtful for a moment. "Buying teddy bears is one, and spending his evenings listening to piano music the last three nights is another. He has a stack of books on his desk on eighteenth-century architecture. And dragging me away from the office to go get your car is a strong indication Webb has succumbed to something more powerful than his business. Nothing"—he stressed the word strongly—"has been more important to Webb than Hunter Construction since he first began the company. To pull me out of the office is something he never would have done before."

"I thought you were partners."

"We are, but it's really Webb's sweat and brains that got the company going. Still keeps it going, for that matter. I had a small accounting firm at one time, and spent a lot of hours away from home, but when Ellen became pregnant with our first child, I knew I had to change my working hours somehow, so I could be home more. Webb knew about my situation, and one day he asked me to come into the business with him. By that time he had built the company into quite a successful operation. At first I thought he was only trying to help me out, that he didn't really need me, but he finally convinced me the operation was getting too big for one man."

"So you agreed to become his partner."

Brad nodded. "I take care of the paper work and sales, which leaves Webb free to oversee the work on the job sites. It's worked out very well for both of us." His smile was ironic. "Especially after I realized he wasn't still trying to run my life. Old habits are hard to break."

Abby was soaking up every word. She encouraged him to continue, needing to hear whatever she could about the man who had taken over her life . . . and her heart.

"I don't understand. Why would Webb try to run your life?"

Leaning back in his chair, Brad debated whether or not to tell Abby about the part of his past he wasn't very proud of. Knowing his brother, he doubted if Webb would ever tell her how he had literally saved Brad's life. But this woman was important to Webb. She should know what kind of man Webb was.

Clearing his throat, he said, "I'm not surprised he hasn't told you. I doubt if he has told anyone." Meeting her intelligent, clear gaze, Brad confessed, "I was an alcoholic by the time I was fifteen. Webb was in his first year of college, and discovered my problem when he was home for spring break. He took over."

His simple statement said so much, but left out even more. "What did he do?"

"Somehow I had managed to hide the drinking from our parents, but when Webb found me drunk as a skunk several times while he was home, he realized I had a definite problem. I still don't know how he convinced our parents to let him take me to his apartment to live with him. Anyway, to make a long story short, he dried me out and watched every move I made. He checked with the school to make sure I didn't skip classes, got me a job after school bagging groceries at a supermarket, and worked my can off at the apartment." He chuckled. "I must have really cramped his style with the ladies, but he never complained."

"How long did you stay with him?" Abby asked quietly.

"For two years. In the summer I worked with him on construction crews and went home when he did. Gradually he got it across to me that I am responsible for my own actions. That lesson, plus the fact that I would have to answer to him if I ever went off the wagon, has kept me stone sober ever since."

"It couldn't have been easy for either one of you."

"We had some good times too," he said, and proceeded to tell her about some of them.

She was laughing about an incident from their childhood when Webb arrived. He came into the kitchen after letting himself into the house, and briefly laid a hand on Abby's shoulder as he passed her. The possessive gesture didn't go unnoticed by his brother, who smiled.

"Did you leave me any coffee?" Webb asked.

"There should be enough for one more cup." Abby didn't bother getting up to get it for him, knowing he preferred to wait on himself.

He leaned one hip against the counter as he sipped his coffee. "I left your keys on the table in the hall," he said to Abby.

"Okay. Thanks. Do you want something to eat?" she asked, indicating the plate of pastries on the table.

"No, thanks. That's Brad's idea of breakfast, not mine. He sneaks junk food whenever Ellen isn't around."

Brad took exception to that remark. "You're going to make Abby think I'm afraid of my wife."

Webb chuckled. "One thing I've learned about Abby is, she thinks for herself."

"You managed to eat quite a few of the rolls Maudie brought over one morning," she reminded him.

Webb looked at Brad. "She also speaks her mind." Glancing at his watch, he added, "We'd better get going, Brad. Abby has things to do, and so do we."

Brad pushed his chair back. "I'm glad I finally got to meet you, Abby. Have Webb bring you over for dinner some night. My wife would like to meet you too."

There was a look of annoyance on Webb's face, and Abby interpreted it to mean he wasn't pleased his brother was taking their relationship for granted. That theory evaporated as soon as Webb spoke to his brother.

"I'll meet you out at the car," he said firmly.

"I thought you wanted to get going."

"You've been married too long. If you want to embarrass Abby by watching us say good-bye properly, stick around."

"I gotcha." Grinning at her, Brad said, "Sorry, Abby. I wasn't thinking."

As soon as Brad left the kitchen, Abby was pulled out of her chair and into Webb's arms. His breath was warm, with a hint of coffee, as he spoke against her lips. "You don't know how hard it was for me to leave you this morning."

His head lowered and his mouth closed over hers. A rush of heat flowed through her. She raised herself on her toes to get closer to him, to deepen the kiss, as hungry for the intimate contact as he. His arms tightened around her, crushing her breasts against his chest, and her lower body melded to his.

She was floating in a sea of weakness as he deepened the kiss, fusing them together. His hands moved down her back to cup her buttocks, bringing her against his hard body. A soft, yearning sound came from deep in her throat.

"Ah, Abby," he breathed against her throat. "That's what I needed this morning. To feel you against me and to hear those soft sounds you make when you're aroused."

He loosened his hold on her reluctantly and transferred his hands to her shoulders as he gazed into her eyes. "Don't look at me like that, Abby, or I might be tempted to make Brad wait out in the truck all morning."

"He thinks you're sleeping with me."

"I am." His fingers soothed and caressed her shoulders and arms, as he felt her tremble. "I like sleeping with you."

"That's not what I meant."

"I know." His smile was soft and sensual, his eyes dark. "I like to make love to you too. To be honest, I hardly think of anything else, especially after the afternoon on the raft."

Her breath caught when she saw the deep hunger in his eyes. "He thinks our relationship is . . . something other than it is."

"Brad knows exactly what our relationship is. You're the only one who doesn't seem to know." He dropped his hands completely. "Duty calls. Yours and mine. Walk me to the door."

Before opening the door, he kissed her again. "What time are you through with your class?"

She wasn't aware of the regret in her eyes now

that he was leaving her, but Webb saw it. "Eleven," she said.

He nodded, kissed her again, and went out the door.

Brad pulled out of Abby's driveway the moment Webb shut the door. As he drove away, he said, "She's not what I expected."

When the truck barely missed a parked car, Webb wished he had offered to take the wheel. His brother always drove as if he had just entered a demolition derby. "What did you expect?"

Turning the wheel sharply to avoid two garbage cans left by the side of the road, Brad replied, "I don't know. A blonde with big bazooms and the IQ of a gnat, I suppose."

"Thanks a lot," Webb growled. First Turk and now Brad.

"You're welcome." Placing his hand on the horn, Brad blasted several times to warn a boy on a bicycle to move over. "I like this one. When are you going to bring her over to the house?"

"We have a few things to work out between us before—Brad, dammit! You almost hit that old lady crossing the street."

"She moves real quick for her age, doesn't she? Talk about old ladies. You're becoming one every time you ride with me." Bringing the conversation back to its original subject, he said, "I saw her face when you came into the kitchen, and also the way you touched her. It seems to me the basics have already been established between you. So what's the problem?"

"I have a few dragons to slay."

Brad took his eyes off the road to stare blankly at his brother. "Excuse me?"

Webb hissed in alarm. "Lord almighty! Watch the road!" When Brad obeyed, Webb clarified his odd statement. "She wants to get her thesis finished so she can get her master's degree, and I'm going to help her. I want the damn thing out of the way. In the process, I want to prove to her she can trust me, lean on me. She's never had anyone to depend on for any length of time, and I have to show her I'm the one who won't go away."

"So her dragons are hang-ups you plan to slaughter?"

"Something like that."

Brad chuckled.

"What's so funny?"

"Your armor is a little rusty from disuse, isn't it? You've always had a rather cavalier attitude toward women. It's hard to picture you as a knight in shining armor, that's all."

"I admit it's not an easy role to fit into, but for this damsel in distress I'll risk making a damn fool of myself."

More to himself than to his brother, Brad muttered, "Well, I'll be damned."

Abby had been home from class for ten minutes when Webb arrived with a sizable lunch basket. He sat her down at the kitchen table, set a huge hamburger in front of her, and ordered her to eat every bite. He took a carton of milk from the basket and poured her a large glass. For dessert, there was an apple. As soon as she was settled to his satisfaction, he joined her, washing down his hamburger with a can of beer.

While they ate, he asked about her class.

"I've been taking a six-week seminar on period clothing of the eighteenth century as a refresher course. Today was the last class."

"Good. That will give you every morning free to work on your thesis." He picked up his second hamburger. "How did you become interested in the eighteenth century? Why not the era of Tara and Scarlett O'Hara?"

"When I was in high school, our class took a tour of Lynnhaven House in Virginia Beach. The guides were in eighteenth-century costumes and made the 1700s come alive for me. I started haunting the library, soaking up all the information I could."

Webb found it interesting that she had chosen the more rugged period of history, rather than a later century. Perhaps it was because she was so familiar with struggling for survival herself.

"How is the thesis coming?" he asked.

"The first draft is almost finished. I have a few more references to look up, then I can begin typing the final draft."

He met her eyes, a flare of hope kindling deep inside him. "How long will that take?"

She shrugged. "I'm not the world's greatest typist. Probably another week or so, depending on how much time I have."

Determination tightened his jaw and narrowed his eyes. "You'll have the time."

The minute Abby took the last bite of her hamburger, Webb whisked the remains of their meal off the table and told her she had an hour to work on her thesis. He cleared the table and washed the dishes while she gathered her papers and books and spread them out on the table. Once the kitchen was tidied up, Webb sat at the other end of the table with a calculator and some papers he had brought with him.

An hour later, Abby changed into her colonial clothes and Webb drove her to Bristol House. A little after five, he was there to take her home. After pulling into the drive, he reached around to get something off the back seat. He dumped a tissue-wrapped bundle onto her lap, then leaned over her to open the door.

"You've got three hours to work on your thesis," he said, and kissed her briefly. "I'll be back at eight with your dinner; then I'll drive you to the hotel."

Abby didn't get out of the car. "Webb," she asked quietly, "why are you doing this?"

"Because I want to," he said simply.

His answer didn't satisfy her, but she knew it was the only one he was going to give her. When she was in her house, she unwrapped the tissue to uncover the teddy bear she knew was inside. This one was dressed in silver armor, a plastic sword attached to one paw.

For some idiotic reason, she felt like crying. Instead she managed a wavering smile and carefully set the bear with the others on her dresser.

It would be possible to enjoy all the attention he was giving her if she knew what his feelings for her were. He seemed to enjoy being with her. The story Brad had told her proved Webb was a caring man. Did he care for her? If he did, in what way? As a sister, a lover, a friend?

Sighing heavily, she changed into a pair of jeans and a red sweat shirt before settling down to work on her thesis. She forced herself to concentrate on the papers in front of her as her fingers moved over the keyboard of her portable typewriter. She was determined to take advantage of the extra time.

At seven-thirty, Webb marched into her kitchen carrying two large sacks of groceries. He plunked them down on the counter and began to unload them, putting each item away as he took it out of the sack.

"What are you doing?" Abby asked.

He opened the refrigerator and set milk, eggs, and a head of lettuce on a shelf. "Never mind what I'm doing. Keep working."

"But—"

"Leave the practicalities of the twentieth century to me. You're supposed to be in the eighteenth century until eight o'clock."

Fragrant aromas began to float across the small kitchen as Webb prepared a meal for them. Promptly at eight, he told Abby to clear her books off the table. Between the two of them, they had the meal on the table in a short time.

Abby sliced a piece of succulent steak. "This is delicious. You're a good cook."

"Anybody can grill a steak. I managed not to starve when I had an apartment off-campus while I attended college. After I got fed up with frozen dinners and peanut butter, I started cooking for myself."

"Was that when Brad was living with you?"

His fork paused halfway to his mouth. "It sounds like Brad has been rattling one of the family skeletons."

"Do you mind that he told me?"

"No."

"Would you ever have told me?"

"No," he answered bluntly. "It's Brad's skeleton, not mine."

She scanned his face. "What about your skeletons? Do you have any?"

"Not that I know of." He smiled. "It's the clean life I lead."

"Must be," she agreed with a hint of skepticism. "Tell me something. Did helping your brother whet your appetite for doing good deeds?"

"Good deeds? You make me sound like a Boy Scout. I'm the dragon slayer, remember? What good deeds am I supposed to be doing?"

"Cooking my dinner, driving me to Bristol House, picking me up, buying groceries. What would you call all those things if not good deeds?"

"Doing my bit for motherhood."

It was unfortunate that Abby had taken a bite of steak just before he spoke. After she finally caught her breath and stopped coughing, she gasped out, "What?"

"You want a baby," he said matter-of-factly. "You need your degree to get a better job so you can qualify to adopt one. I'm going to make sure you get it. You need time. You're going to have it." He paused, then added, "After you've achieved your goal, we can get to work on mine."

He forestalled anything she might say by glancing at his watch and shoving his chair back. "Time for you to get ready for work."

In a daze, Abby wandered into her bedroom. While she showered and dressed, she thought about what he had said. There had been no emotion in his voice or in his eyes. He had been almost formal as he outlined his campaign. Whatever the reasons were for his gallant efforts on her behalf, she wasn't going to object. She wanted to be with him whenever she could. It was that simple. She was aware of the hazards and accepted them. The more she learned about him, the longer she was with him, the deeper the pain would be when he had tired of being the good knight. She would have to deal with that when it happened.

She had mixed feelings about finishing her thesis now. Once it was completed, would he consider his mission accomplished?

Whatever the outcome, she was going to take advantage of the opportunity to be with him. Life hadn't handed her many bonuses. She was going to grab and hang on to this one as long as she could.

That evening, she was aware of Webb sitting at a table while she played the piano. Brad had mentioned something about Webb's having been at the hotel the previous three nights. She had meant to ask him about that, but it had slipped her mind. She was afraid he would be bored silly listening to piano music for hours on end, but he didn't seem to mind.

Later he took her home, and, to her disappointment, only kissed her briefly and left. She had expected him to come inside, had wanted him to spend the night with her. He had awakened her sleeping passion that Sunday at the lake, and she wanted him again.

On Saturday she worked on her thesis all day, taking time out to eat the lunch Webb fixed. At dinnertime he arrived with a huge pizza covered with sausage, mushrooms, and extra cheese. As soon as they had polished it off, he stood, saying he had to leave.

Abby silently followed him to the door. She didn't want him to go. She wanted—perhaps foolishly—more of him, more than just his company when he ate with her or chauffeured her to work. How could she get him to stay?

At the door, Webb turned to her, his mouth a tight line, his muscles taut. She was so lovely, and the heat and aroma of her body seemed to float around him, ensnaring him. Damn, he wanted her.

He didn't know how much more of this he could take.

"Good night, Abby," he said. He raised his hand to touch her, just to stroke her cheek, then thought better of it. But before he could pull back, she took his hand and brought it up to her throat, her gaze locked with his. Her fingers tightened around his wrist as slowly, relentlessly, she slid his hand down the front of her shirt, and inside it.

He groaned her name hoarsely as he felt her soft flesh under his hand. His fingers grazed the hard tip of her breast. "Abby, no," he murmured in a choked voice, unable to remove his hand from her warm, silky skin.

The tremor in his voice and his caressing fingers gave Abby the courage to slide her other hand behind his head to bring it down to hers, needing the reassurance of his reactions, needing him.

His head spun crazily as his mouth took hers hungrily, with a desperation beyond anything he had ever experienced. He shouldn't be touching her, wanting her. He would only kiss her. Just this once. His tongue found hers, then thrust into her mouth with the intimate motion his body was aching to imitate.

Abby arched her back to bring her body against his, and was distressed when his other hand clamped down on her waist to keep her away from his aroused lower body. He was still resisting her . . . and it hurt. He was giving her conflicting signals, his mouth devouring her while he kept their bodies apart.

Suddenly he broke away from her, slowly withdrawing his hand from inside her shirt, his jaw clenched with an effort at self-control.

"I have to go," he said hoarsely.

For a long moment, she could only stare at him

There was a fine sheen of perspiration on his skin. Not wanting to make a bigger fool of herself than she already had, she opened the door, turning her head away as he left. Once he was gone she quietly closed the door.

She had brazenly offered herself, but he had turned her down. He had kissed her as though he had been starved for the taste of her, yet had drawn away from her.

She was confused and bewildered by his physical withdrawal from her. Why was he torturing her this way? And why was she letting him?

Webb's thoughts were no more comforting as he drove home. When he had first conceived this plan of taking over the mundane daily tasks to give Abby more free time, he hadn't considered his compulsive need for her. Even now the thought of her slender body under his and the satin heat of her was drugging his mind, making him ache for her. His noble decision not to make love to her was killing him by degrees.

The vulnerable look in her eyes just before he left her had almost made him reach for her, but he had fought against it. He had to have all of her, not just her passion. And he would . . . if he survived.

On Sunday Webb didn't stay to share a meal with Abby. At lunchtime, after he saw that she was sitting down to eat the bowl of chili he had set in front of her, he left abruptly. She shoved the bowl away, but not because she feared the chili would dissolve her fillings. She had lost her appetite with him gone.

He had spoken two words to her, "Sit" and "Eat"; then he had marched from the kitchen and out the door. His attitude was beginning to annoy her, crowding out the hurt to make way for a rousing, healthy anger.

That evening he brought an assortment of dishes from a Chinese restaurant. When it looked as if he were just going to dump them on the table and take off again, Abby rebelled.

"No!"

He stopped in the kitchen doorway and turned to look at her. "What?"

"You aren't leaving."

He was captivated by her flashing green eyes and the proud tilt of her chin. "I'm not?"

"No, you're not. I'm not some helpless invalid who needs Meals on Wheels. You either sit down and eat with me or take all this with you."

Her outrage made him smile with tender affection. Against his better judgment, he came back into the room, stopping in front of her.

Placing his hands on either side of her neck, he allowed himself the luxury of stroking the satiny skin along her jawline before lowering his hands to his sides. "Abby, I can't stay."

"Why not?"

"Because if I do, we won't spend our time in the kitchen among the egg rolls and egg-drop soup. I want you very badly. I can't be around you without wanting to make love to you."

"Would that be so awful?"

"I'm trying to do the right thing by leaving you alone." His voice was tight with strain.

"Right for who, you or me?" she asked quietly.

"For us."

"There is no us," she said bitterly.

His hand reached out to grasp her arm when she turned away from him.

"The hell there isn't. Us means a combination of two or more people." His fingers caught her chin, forcing her to meet his eyes. "In case you haven't noticed, you and I make one helluva combination. That makes an us, as in you and me together."

She protested, unsatisfied with his theory. "But—"

Suddenly his hands moved to her waist and she was lifted up onto the kitchen counter. He made a space for himself between her legs, and his hands slid under her shirt to find her soft skin.

His breath was warm against her mouth as he said huskily, "You shouldn't have made me touch you, Abby. I'm barely managing to hang on to some semblance of control every time I just look at you. Touching you makes it almost impossible."

Her arms went around his neck. "I want you to touch me," she murmured against his mouth. "I've missed you."

Webb closed his eyes as an explosive emotion ripped through him. To be needed by her was almost as powerful as his need for her. "I have to kiss you, Abby. I'll go out of my mind if I don't." He gave a short, mirthless laugh. "Hell, I'll go out of my mind if I do."

His mouth covered hers, parting her lips, tasting her, loving her with a freedom he wouldn't allow his body to have. His callused hands glided over her cool skin as he broke away from her mouth to press his lips against her neck.

Her thighs gripped his hips convulsively as his lips foraged and feasted on the vulnerable spot below her ear. Her hands abandoned his tense back to grasp his hair and bring his mouth back to hers. She was eager to please him, knowing she would receive pleasure in return.

Impatient to feel his long, hard body along the length of hers, she tried to move off the counter. His hands clamped down on her waist to prevent her.

"No," he muttered against her neck. "Don't move. Just give me a minute."

His taut body shuddered under her hands, and she realized the extent of his struggle to control his desire for her.

He held her for a few more precious minutes while his breathing became less ragged. Then he drew his arms away. He met her troubled gaze. "Abby, I've discovered I'm a very selfish man."

His fingers came up to her mouth to stop her protest. "Yes, I am. I don't want anything between us. Your degree is important to you, and all your attention should be focused on it. I understand that. You've worked so hard to get where you are, and I can't stand in the way now."

She pushed his hand away, holding on to his wrist. "But you aren't in the way. My Lord, you've been doing so much to make sure I have spare time to finish my thesis."

He backed away several steps, needing the distance from her. "Right now the thesis is between us. Even though you don't think you would regret any time taken away from reaching your goal, I'm not going to take that chance. When we went to the lake, you said that day was the only one you could take off. I've accepted that. I'm staying away from you to give you the space and time to finish that damn thesis."

"And after the thesis is done?"

"Then we'll have time for us. I want you to give all your attention to me, without any competition." He gave her a half-smile and said softly, "Eat your dinner and get to work. I'll see you tomorrow."

"Well, damn," Abby muttered under her breath as Webb shut the door on his way out, leaving her alone again.

Suddenly, she narrowed her eyes with determination. Ignoring the food he had brought, she yanked open the back door and raced down the steps.

Ira answered the door. Maudie was seated at the kitchen table sorting through an overflowing recipe box.

Abby's greeting consisted of a heated, "Men are impossible."

Ira blinked and immediately left the room like a scared rabbit.

Maudie calmly accepted Abby's assessment of the male gender, commenting, "They have their moments."

Abby sat down and outlined for Maudie the martyrdom act Webb was pulling on her. "He thinks he's doing me this gigantic favor by leaving me alone so I can finish my thesis. The man is driving me crackers."

Maudie smiled. "I thought you wanted to get your thesis done as soon as possible."

"I did. I do. It's not as important as it was before, though." Leaning her arms on the table, Abby added, "He has some idiotic notion the completed thesis is more important than . . . Well, never mind. I have an idea about how to shake him up a little, but I'll need your help."

The recipes were forgotten. "You have it."

"Good. Now, this is what I have planned. . . ."

Ten

Webb had given Abby a powerful incentive to finish her thesis, and she immediately set about doing just that. Occasionally nibbling on an egg roll, she tore into the eighteenth century with a vengeance. The typewriter clattered continuously as page after page was typed. A cup of steaming coffee was always within reach as Abby's fingers diligently pecked at the keys.

By one o'clock in the morning, she had to get up from the table to walk around, massaging her aching muscles as she stretched her legs. A few minutes later, she sat back down again and resumed her work. It took the rest of the night to finish typing the hundred-and-twenty-one-page document. At six o'clock in the morning, she set the alarm for nine o'clock and fell into bed.

The minute the alarm rang, Abby turned it off and hopped out of bed. After a quick shower, she pulled on her jeans and a yellow sweater, and gathered her hair back into a ponytail. In spite of only getting a few hours of sleep, she was full of energy. There was a lot to do and she was determined to get every single thing done. Her future happiness depended on it.

The knot of apprehension in her stomach made it impossible for her to think of eating any breakfast. She managed to drink a glass of milk, but that was all she dared have.

First on her list was to have a copy made of the thesis. Then she would take it to her adviser at the university. She set it on the table by the door to get it out of the way while she cleaned off the kitchen table. Her notes, notebooks, and reference books all went into a cardboard box to be stored in her closet.

Grabbing her purse, car keys, and the thesis, she hurried over to the Burrowses. She needed to use the phone and see if Maudie was ready for their shopping trip.

Her first phone call was to Webb, to tell him not to come to her house at noon to insist that she eat lunch and later to drive her to Bristol House. He was out of the office, but Brad picked up the phone after the secretary told him who it was.

"Hi, Abby. It's Brad. You'll have to settle for me. Webb isn't here right now. What's up?"

Maybe it was better to handle the change of plans through Brad, Abby thought. Then there wouldn't be any arguments from Webb. "Could you get a message to Webb before noon?"

"Sure. No problem. I can call him on his beeper. What's the message?"

"Tell him he doesn't have to stop by at noon. Ask him to come to the house at seven tonight instead."

"Got it." After a momentary pause, Brad added, "Ah . . . Abby, I think I should warn you that Webb is not going to take kindly to having his plans changed. He's made it a point to clear his schedule to make time for you."

"I know, but there are certain things I have to do today that are important. He'll understand later tonight."

Brad chuckled. "Heaven help him. This sounds like one of those times when a mere male doesn't stand a chance in hell if a woman changes the plot."

Abby ignored his remark. "Will you be sure he gets the message before noon?"

"You got it." Still chuckling, Brad hung up the phone, a broad grin on his face. He had the feeling his brother was in for one hell of a frustrating day and an interesting evening.

After making sure another one of the docents could fill in for her that day, Abby then phoned the administrator of Bristol House and informed him she wouldn't be there that afternoon, without giving any definite reason. This was the first time she had not shown up for work, and since she had found a replacement, the administrator went along with her request.

As soon as she hung up the phone it rang. It was Webb, calling from a pay phone. There was the sound of traffic in the background, but his voice came through loud and clear. So did his displeasure.

"What's going on?" he asked. "Why don't you want me to take you to Bristol House?"

She'd been afraid this would happen. Everything had been working out so well thus far. "I have some running around to do today, and it's not necessary for you to waste your time carting me around."

"Abby," he said sternly, "I don't feel I'm wasting my time. What do you have to do? Maybe I can do the errands for you, and you'll have the extra time to work on your thesis."

She didn't want to give anything away, so she was purposely vague. "They're things I have to do myself. Did Brad tell you about coming over tonight at seven?"

"I didn't understand that either. I had planned to fix your dinner earlier."

"Seven would be better. Look, I have to go. I'll see you at seven."

Quickly hanging up the phone, Abby took a deep breath. So far so good. She would have to keep her fingers crossed that Webb would abide by her request, and not be stubborn and come over at the time he had originally planned. It would ruin everything.

Picking up the phone again, she dialed the hotel and talked to the lounge manager. He wasn't at all pleased to hear she wouldn't be in to work that evening, but she ignored his complaints. At least he hadn't fired her, but she was past caring even if he had.

It took several hours for Abby and Maudie to accumulate the supplies Abby needed before Webb arrived that evening. Maudie was inexhaustible as she gamely accompanied Abby to the art-supply store, the grocery store, and the stationery and card shop. Some of Maudie's suggestions were so outrageous, Abby ended up laughing most of the time they were together. The older woman was clearly having the time of her life.

Ira made himself scarce when they returned to Maudie's house. He wasn't about to contribute to the inevitable downfall of a fellow male.

Over innumerable pots of tea, the two women worked at Maudie's dining-room table. By five o'clock they were able to sit back and enjoy one last, leisurely cup of tea, satisfied with their afternoon's work. Abby turned down Maudie's dinner invitation. She still had a couple of other things to arrange before Webb arrived.

A few minutes before seven, Webb parked his car in the driveway, behind Abby's car. If the slamming of his car door was an accurate indicator, his disposition was not a rosy one. He scowled as he started toward her front door, but then, several feet from the porch, he stopped and stared.

One of the teddy bears he had given Abby was sitting on the bottom step. A sign was propped up between his paws. Edging closer to the sign, Webb read the block lettering: "Please go around to the back of the house."

Puzzled, he started around the corner of the house. He was met by another bear, this one holding a cardboard arrow pointing the way toward the back. Several others were positioned along his path, directing him. At the gate, Beau Bear waited. He was without his fishing rod, but held a sign that read: "Come on in and join the party."

Webb lifted the latch and slowly pushed the gate open, wondering what he would find. Completely intrigued, he forgot he had been furious with Abby for changing the day's plans. After taking two steps, he stopped.

In the middle of the lawn was a white blanket surrounded by white sacks. They were weighted down, and in the center of each was a lighted candle. The rest of the teddy bears were arranged around the edge of the blanket, a paper party hat perched on the top of each fuzzy head.

There was a silver platter of cheese, salami, and crackers next to an ice bucket containing a bottle of champagne.

In the middle of all this sat Abby.

Webb could only stare at the lovely picture she made in the fading light with the candles illuminating her. Her hair had been arranged in a complicated coil on top of her head, complementing her elegant black crepe de chine dress.

Abby tried to look calm and serene as she returned Webb's stunned gaze. So far everything was going as planned, but so much depended on his reaction.

Finally he walked toward her. "You should have told me this was going to be a formal evening," he said, glancing down at his tan slacks and navy shirt. "I would have worn a dinner jacket."

She shifted over to make room for him next to her. "I wanted this to be a surprise."

"It was that." Bending his long legs, he sat down beside her. One foot accidentally knocked over a bear and he set it upright. "What's the occasion?"

"I'll tell you after you open the champagne."

Webb figured it was easier to go along with whatever she was up to than to keep asking questions. He reached for the bottle and popped the cork, quickly lifting one of the crystal champagne goblets to catch the bubbly sparkling liquid.

He filled the glasses and handed her one, patiently waiting for whatever was next.

She raised her glass and made a toast. "To a Teddy Bear's Picnic."

Her glass clinked against his.

After taking a sip, Abby made another toast. "To one completed thesis."

He had raised his glass automatically to touch hers, but her words stopped him. His gaze searched her face. "You finished it?"

She nodded. "During the night. I dropped it off this morning."

Webb took a healthy swallow of champagne. He felt as if a heavy weight had been lifted from his shoulders . . . and the exhilaration didn't come from the champagne he was drinking. Now he had all the time in the world.

"So what happens now?" he asked.

Abby had the feeling he wasn't referring to her completed thesis. But she pretended that was what he was talking about. "I wait to hear if it's accepted."

He nodded. "Then what?"

She frowned. He knew what her plans were. "Then I . . ." She couldn't remember what she was going to say, because his hand was stroking the fabric covering her thigh. "What are you doing?"

"This is the same dress you wore the night you had the flat tire. Aren't you afraid you'll spill something on it before you go to the hotel tonight?"

His hand had reached the top of her thigh, and his thumb was creating an erotic friction of cloth against sensitive skin.

Her voice was slightly shaky as she answered. "I won't be going to the hotel tonight."

His hand stilled, but he didn't remove it. "You aren't going to work tonight? Why?"

"I decided to take the night off."

There was a strange glitter in his eyes. "You wore this dress for me?"

She smiled. "I thought we would celebrate in style."

"Ah, Abby. I don't know how to break this to you, but this looks more like a seduction scene than a celebration party."

Inside she was quaking, but it was now or never. "If that bothers you, you don't have to stay. The bears and I can have a party by ourselves."

Her chin had lifted in that familiar proud gesture that never failed to send heat throughout his body. "You've gone to a lot of trouble for a party for some bears. The least I can do is stay." He gave her a disturbingly sensual smile. "I have to stick around to see how you plan to carry out the seduction part. I'm all for it, of course, and will help in any way I can."

She should have known he wouldn't stay on the course she had set. "That's very generous of you. What if I told you this was only a party to celebrate completing my thesis?"

"I would be disappointed. I don't mean I'm not pleased the blasted thesis is done. I couldn't be happier." He picked up a piece of cheese and placed it on a cracker. "Don't mind me. Go right ahead with your plans."

This wasn't going quite right. Her whole strategy had been geared for a surprise assault, hoping to catch him off-balance. Instead, she was the one stumbling around trying to find her equilibrium. His responses weren't what she had expected, so she would have to improvise. He was entirely too sure of himself.

Raising her glass, she said, "I have another toast to make."

He finished munching on the cracker and lifted his own glass. "I'm ready."

"To my Ph.D."

"Your *what*?"

She barely controlled her elation at finally getting a reaction. "I thought that since I've got all the paper work out of the way for my master's, I would go on to get a doctorate."

"Well, think again." Visions of the torture of the last week darted through Webb's mind, making him cringe. The thought of going through it again for an even longer period of time . . . "What about all those plans for becoming an instructor at the university so you can adopt a baby?"

"I could still do that and take classes at night."

"If your plan is to drive me stark, raving mad, let me be the first to congratulate you. You've succeeded."

"You don't like the idea?" she asked innocently.

"I hate it if it means a repeat of the last week." He glared at her. "I'll do it all again if I have to, but I won't like it."

A spark of hope began to glow inside her. "You will?"

"Yes, but I warn you. A man can be expected to take only so many cold showers." He tossed his empty glass into the grass, clearly at the end of his rope. "No, dammit. I've had it. Don't look now, lady, but your dragon slayer just fell off his charger."

Her glass was yanked out of her hand and flung over his shoulder. He grabbed her arms and lowered her to the blanket, toppling several bears in the process. This time he didn't bother to set them upright.

His weight crushed her into the blanket-covered grass. Her body was soft and pliant under his as he devoured her mouth, staking a claim while testifying to his desire for her. His urgent need was no longer disguised or hidden from her as he sought the velvety warmth of her mouth.

His hands swept over her waist and hips, seductively outlined by her black dress. It had been too long since he had allowed himself the freedom to touch her as he wanted to touch her, to feel her come gloriously alive under him, to hear her soft sounds of arousal.

Desperation mixed with blatant male hunger as he tore his mouth from hers to trail his lips over her face and neck.

"Don't put me too far down on your list of priorities, Abby," he growled. "I won't stay there. I have to know where I fit in your scheme of things. In front of your Ph.D. or behind it."

She let her fingers trail over his firm jaw. "In place of."

Her quiet, unexpected declaration brought his head up. His eyes were dark and wide with shock.

Slowly easing his body off her and propping himself up on one elbow, he searched her face. "Abby?" he asked raggedly. "What is this? Some kind of test?" There was a rough edge to his voice. "Let's tease Webb to see how far we can push him?"

"Webb, I love you."

He stared at her, completely stunned for an instant. Then his hands were cupping her face, his fingers weaving through her hair. "Oh, Abby," he muttered hoarsely. "I didn't think I'd ever hear those words from you."

She shoved aside the flicker of disappointment that he hadn't immediately returned the sentiment. Maybe he never would.

She loosened her arms from around his neck. "I wasn't sure you wanted to hear them."

He saw the vulnerability in her eyes, and his hands were gentle as he took her in his arms. "Abby, of course I wanted to hear you say you love me. My Lord, I've been acting like a beggar at your door, accepting whatever crumbs you threw my way. Why do you think I was willing to put your desires ahead of my own?"

It was Abby's turn to stare at him.

"Darling," he murmured as he drew back enough to be able to see her eyes. "I'm madly, insanely, desperately in love with you. Forever and longer. I want to come home to you, wake up each morning to find your glorious hair spread out on the pillow beside me, and grow old and crotchety alongside you."

His fingers searched through the mass of her hair, dropping the pins into the grass. The silken hair fell around her shoulders, and he combed his fingers through it, loving the sensual feel of it against his skin.

"I love your hair." His hand stroked her shoulder, then down over her breasts to her waist and hips. His smile was soft and sexy. "I'm rather fond of the rest of you too."

"Webb," she whispered. "Make love to me. Make me believe you really love me."

He rolled onto his back, his strong arms bringing her with him. The zipper at the back of her dress slid down to the base of her spine. "You look beautiful in this dress, but you will be even more beautiful without it."

Her hands were shaking as she worked loose the buttons on his shirt. Then she smoothed her palms over his firm, muscular chest and heard his quick intake of air. She was amazed she could so arouse him with her touch.

A rush of heat flowed through her as his rough hands slid over her smooth, bare back. She could feel his aroused body beneath hers and she pressed her hips into his. He groaned with aching pleasure against her mouth.

Feeling his control shredding into tatters, he swept her dress down over her hips.

While she could still think, she murmured, "Don't you think we should go inside?"

"I plan to be eventually," he said, changing the meaning of her words. Her black bra joined her dress on the blanket. "I want to see your skin by candlelight. No one can see us."

His mouth found her breast and Abby forgot about everything but Webb and the growing ache in her body. "It's been one hell of a week, Abby," he murmured. "I thought I would die from wanting you so badly."

His lips lingered on the tempting rise of her breast, his tongue flicking across her hard nipple. His name came out in a shaky sigh as his mouth closed over the tip, creating blazing fires in both of them.

"It's been too long, darling," he breathed against her heated flesh. "I have to have you now. I need you to make me whole again."

After removing the rest of her clothing and his own, he reversed their positions, sliding intimately between her legs.

Before he took her completely, he said huskily, "Marry me, Abby. Have my babies, live with me. I love you so much. Please marry me."

Unbearable pleasure surged through her as she felt the waiting power of his hard body against her own. "In my heart, I already have."

The world exploded in fragments all around her as he plunged inside her, joining them in love and commitment. Ecstasy tugged at her with each passionate movement. All the lonely nights and empty days faded, to be replaced by a wealth of sensations as he took her to the glorious land of love and need.

Finally she had someone of her own to love and who loved her, now and for the rest of her time on earth.

THE EDITOR'S CORNER

We have Valentine's Day presents galore for you next month . . . hearts, flowers, chuckles, and a sentimental tear or two. We haven't wrapped your presents in the traditional colors of the special holiday for lovers, though. Rather, we're presenting them in a spectrum of wonderful earth colors from vibrant, exhilarating Green to sinfully rich chocolate Brown. (Apologies to Billie and Sandra for using their last names this way, but I couldn't resist!)

First, in **MAKIN' WHOOPEE,** LOVESWEPT #182, by—of course—Billie Green, you'll discover the perfect Valentine's Day heroine, Sara Love. Ms. Love's business partner (and sweet nemesis) is the wickedly good-looking Charlie Sanderson. These two charmers have been waging a long silent battle to repress their true feelings for one another. He has built for himself a reputation as "Good Time Charlie," the swinging bachelor; she has built walls around her emotions, pouring all her energies into the business. An ill-fated trip to inspect a piece of property is the catalyst for the erosion of their defenses, but it isn't until a little bundle of joy makes an astonishing appearance that these two humorous and heartwarming and sexy people come together at last . . . and forever. With all the freshness, optimism, and excitement we associate with the green of springtime, Billie creates in **MAKIN' WHOOPEE** two characters whose love story you'll long remember.

TANGLES, LOVESWEPT #183, by Barbara Boswell, is a story that dazzled me so much I see it as painted in brilliant yellows and golds. Barbara's heroine, Krista Conway, is a highpowered divorce lawyer who is as beautiful as she is brainy. And to hero Logan Moore, the new judge who is trying Krista's case, she is the most seductive lady he's ever laid eyes on. Now Krista may appear hard as nails, but beneath her beautiful and sophisticated exterior is a

(*continued*)

tender woman who yearns for a man to love and a family to care for. Logan is one heck of a sexy widower with three delightful children . . . and he's a man who is badly misled by Krista's image and wildly confused by his compelling need for her. In a series of events that by turns sizzle with love and romance and sear with emotional intensity, the **TANGLES** these two wonderful people find themselves in begin to unravel to an unexpectedly beautiful ending. Bravo, Barbara Boswell!

The warm earth colors of orange, pale to dusky, had to have been on the palette of Anne and Ed Kolaczyk as they created **SULTRY NIGHTS,** LOVE-SWEPT #184. In this poignant romance of love lost and love regained, we encounter Rachel Anders years after her passionate affair with Ben Healey. One brilliant, erotic, tenderly emotional summer was all Rachel and Ben had together before he had to leave town. Rachel lived on in pained loss, faced with Ben's silence, and comforted only by the legacy of their passion, a beloved daughter. When they meet again, the attraction between them is fired to even greater heat than they'd known in their youth. But Rachel's secret still will come between them until they find their own path to a love that time could not destroy. Ablaze with intensity, **SULTRY NIGHTS** is a captivating love story.

Sandra Brown is a remarkably talented and hard-working author who seems phenomenal to me in the way she keeps topping herself in the creation of one wonderful love story after another. And here comes another of her delectably sensual love stories, **SUNNY CHANDLER'S RETURN,** LOVESWEPT #185. I referred above to "sinfully rich chocolate." I must have written those words because unconsciously I was still under the sway of a very short, but never-to-be forgotten episode in this book involving triple dipped strawberries. (See if you don't delight in that scene as much as I did.) And speaking of people who are

(*continued*)

phenomenal in topping themselves, I must mention Barbara Alpert who writes all the splendid back cover copy for our LOVESWEPTs. Her description of Sandra's next book is so terrific that I'm going to give you a sneak preview of the back cover copy. Here's what Barbara wrote.

"The whispers began when she entered the ballroom— and every male eye in the place was caught by the breathtakingly lovely spitfire with the slightly shady reputation. Ty Beaumont knew a heartbreaker when he saw one—and also knew that nothing and nobody could keep him from making her his inside a week's time. He'd bet a case of Wild Turkey on it! Sunny heard his devil's voice drawl in her ear, and couldn't help but notice the man was far too handsome for his own good, but his fierce ardor sparked hers, and his "I'll have you naked yet" smile caused a kind of spontaneous combustion that nothing could quench. Private torments had sent both Ty and Sunny racing from the past, but would revealing their dark secrets let them face the future together?"

We think next month offers you a particularly exciting quartet of LOVESWEPTs, and we hope you enjoy each one immensely.

With every good wish,

Carolyn Nichols

Carolyn Nichols
  Editor
LOVESWEPT
Bantam Books, Inc.
666 Fifth Avenue
New York, NY 10103

*Heirs to a great dynasty, the Delaney
brothers were united by blood, united by
devotion to their rugged land . . . and
known far and wide as*

THE SHAMROCK
TRINITY

Bantam's bestselling LOVESWEPT romance line built its reputation on quality and innovation. Now, a remarkable and unique
event in romance publishing comes from the same source: THE
SHAMROCK TRINITY, three daringly original novels written by
three of the most successful women's romance writers today. Kay
Hooper, Iris Johansen, and Fayrene Preston have created a trio
of books that are dynamite love stories bursting with strong,
fascinating male and female characters, deeply sensual love scenes,
the humor for which LOVESWEPT is famous, and a deliciously
fresh approach to romance writing.

*THE SHAMROCK TRINITY—Burke, York, and
Rafe: Powerful men . . . rakes and charmers . . .
they needed only love to make their lives complete.*

☐ *RAFE, THE MAVERICK by Kay Hooper*

Rafe Delaney was a heartbreaker whose ebony eyes held laughing
devils and whose lilting voice could charm any lady—or any
horse—until a stallion named Diablo left him in the dust. It took
Maggie O'Riley to work her magic on the impossible horse . . .
and on his bold owner. Maggie's grace and strength made Rafe
yearn to share the raw beauty of his land with her, to teach her
the exquisite pleasure of yielding to the heat inside her. Maggie
was stirred by Rafe's passion, but would his reputation and her
ambition keep their kindred spirits apart?   (21786 • $2.50)

 LOVESWEPT

☐ YORK, THE RENEGADE by Iris Johansen

Some men were made to fight dragons, Sierra Smith thought when she first met York Delaney. The rebel brother had roamed the world for years before calling the rough mining town of Hell's Bluff home. Now, the spirited young woman who'd penetrated this renegade's paradise had awakened a savage and tender possessiveness in York: something he never expected to find in himself. Sierra had known loneliness and isolation too—enough to realize that York's restlessness had only to do with finding a place to belong. Could she convince him that love was such a place, that the refuge he'd always sought was in her arms?

(21787 • $2.50)

☐ BURKE, THE KINGPIN by Fayrene Preston

Cara Winston appeared as a fantasy, racing on horseback to catch the day's last light—her silver hair glistening, her dress the color of the Arizona sunset . . . and Burke Delaney wanted her. She was on his horse, on his land: she would have to belong to him too. But Cara was quicksilver, impossible to hold, a wild creature whose scent was midnight flowers and sweet grass. Burke had always taken what he wanted, by willing it or fighting for it; Cara cherished her freedom and refused to believe his love would last. Could he make her see he'd captured her to have and hold forever?

(21788 • $2.50)